This special signed edition of

AUTUMN PROSE,
WINTER VERSE

is limited to 100 copies

Mark Steensland

34

This is copy

Autumn Prose,
Winter Verse

Autumn Prose, Winter Verse

MARK STEENSLAND

Contents

Autumn Prose, Winter Verse

Lovecraft's Pillow

THE HAIR ON MARTIN HALE'S NECK PRICKLED WHEN HE heard the basement door open. Glancing up the cellar steps, he waited for Alice, his wife, to appear in the darkness at the top of the stairs. He could almost imagine the air was tinged with a hint of sulfurous fumes. After a moment's hesitation, she started down the stairs, making each step creak beneath her weight. And with every step, the tension in Martin's shoulders coiled tighter and tighter. His hands, poised over the keyboard, began to shake a little as his wife stepped into the light and approached his tiny work area in the corner next to the furnace.

"How's the story coming along?" she asked, but her tone of voice was so flat Martin got the clear impression she didn't really care how anything was coming along.

"Slowly," Martin said, clenching his hands into fists above the keyboard of his laptop to keep them from shaking.

"Well," Alice said. "The mail came."

Martin caught the curling sneer on her upper lip.

"Did I hear back from—"

Before he could finish, his wife dropped an envelope onto the keyboard. The sound of the impact made him jump, and the edge of the

envelope hit the K and L keys so both letters suddenly appeared on
the screen in the middle of the story he'd been working on.

"The electric company?" she said.

Then she plunked another envelope down on top of the first.

"Or the gas company?"

A third envelope landed on top of the pile.

"Or the credit card company? Who were you waiting to hear from,
Martin?"

Martin stared up at her, unable to speak for a moment. After a
brief hesitation, she dropped a final envelope onto the keyboard.

"Or were you looking for this?" She paused, and for an instant,
Martin was filled with hope before she added, "It's from the IRS."

Martin's shoulders sagged as he stared at the pile of bad news.
A cold sensation tightened around his chest, and his throat felt
unbelievably dry. He took a shallow breath, but the musty air in the
basement where he had his writing office almost choked him.

"Nothing from—"

"—*Cemetery Dance Magazine*?" Alice was no longer even trying
to keep the disdain off her face or out of her voice as she held up an
envelope with the *Cemetery Dance* logo for a return address. Before
handing it to him, she held the letter up to the desk light and shook it
from side to side. Through the thin paper, he could see a single sheet
of paper. "But it doesn't look like there's a check in there."

Martin reached across the desk and grabbed the envelope from
her. His pulse was racing hard in his neck as he tore open the envelope and took out the letter. After only a quick glance, his eyes came
to rest on the last sentence above the editor's signature:

"*We wish you luck placing your story elsewhere.*" Next to that, scrawled
in black ink, was a scribbled message: "*You came really close this time,
Mr. Hale. Please keep trying.*"

Swallowing his disappointment, Martin folded the letter up,
slipped it back into the envelope, and placed it in the bottom drawer

of his desk, where it would molder slowly with the rest of his rejection letters and rejected stories.

"I knew it," Alice said, sounding almost sad as she leaned back and folded her arms across her chest. "You wanna know what I think?"

Shielding his eyes from the glare of the desk light, Martin looked up at her. He knew *exactly* what she was going to say, but he also knew she was going to say it anyway.

"I think you've gotta give it up, Martin. You've been trying to get published for more than ten years now, but you know what? You ain't never gonna get published. Ever." She hesitated, and for a split second, Martin thought she was going to say something positive, but then she added, "And I was a fool to think you ever would."

Almost choking on his suppressed rage and frustration, Martin lowered his gaze and stared at the glowing screen of his laptop.

"I need some inspiration," he said, as much to himself as to her. "Some real inspiration."

"No," Alice said, her high-pitched voice cracking like a whip across his face. "What you need to do is return that laptop we couldn't afford in the first place and go get a *real* job."

"The store won't take it back," he said, his stomach churning with despair. "It's been more than ninety days."

Alice turned and started walking toward the stairs. "Then I guess you'll have to pawn it."

Staring at the glowing computer screen, Martin mumbled, "If you didn't buy so many shoes . . ."

"I heard that," Alice said, not bothering to turn and look at him as she hesitated on the stairs. He jumped when she reached the top and closed the door behind her.

The next morning, with the laptop in its black case slung over his shoulder, Martin walked downtown. It had rained earlier, and everything was still damp. The city streets, at least in this part of Providence, perfectly matched his mood. The piles of litter along the curbs, the boarded-up storefronts with soaped-over windows, the broken parking meters, the stray cats and dogs roaming the alleys, and the vacant lots choked with weeds—*everything* looked as destitute and desolate as Martin was feeling inside at the prospect of actually giving up his dream of becoming a published writer.

The front and sides of the pawnshop were about the only things with any color or life in this part of town. A local artist had painted a Caribbean beach scene with Rastafarians and sunbathers dancing under palm trees with a tropical ocean and sky. The artwork seemed so out of place in such a drab part of the city it almost made Martin smile as he approached the storefront. As he was reaching for the doorknob, the display in the front window caught his eye, and he froze.

"What the—?" he muttered as he leaned close to the window, unable to believe what he was looking at.

It wasn't much—an average-sized blue-and-white-striped pillow with a large brownish stain in the center. It was the sign in front of the pillow that riveted Martin's attention.

Lovecraft's Pillow—$250.00

Martin's breath caught in his chest. He couldn't stop staring at the pillow and the sign. He was afraid it was magical and would disappear the instant he turned away or even blinked. Finally, feeling the weight of the laptop on his shoulder, he grabbed the doorknob and pulled the door open. The bells above the door jingled as he entered.

"*The* Lovecraft?" he asked.

The middle-aged man leaning on the counter with both elbows looked up from his casual perusal of a girlie magazine. He had a toothpick in his mouth, which he kept shifting from one corner to the other as he stared at Martin with a somewhat bewildered look. He seemed almost angry that a customer had dared interrupt his day.

"H. P. Lovecraft?" Martin said, barely able to contain his excitement. "The writer? That's *really* his pillow in the window?"

He was standing close to the display. Suddenly fearful that it would be gone, he turned to glance at the pillow again.

Amazingly, it was still there.

It looked so mundane, but the rush of excitement that ran like an electric current through Martin was far from mundane.

"'S what the guy who pawned it said," the pawnshop owner replied with an *I-could-give-a-shit* shrug.

"May I?" Martin asked, his voice trembling with reverence as he indicated the pillow with a quick nod of his head.

"Whatever," the pawnshop owner said as he sauntered over to the window display, snatched up the pillow, and handed it to Martin.

For a moment or two, Martin hesitated to take it from the man. He felt it might be a little bit sacrilegious or something even to touch it, but when the store owner appeared to be getting impatient, Martin took the pillow from him, letting it rest on his opened palms.

"Just think," he said, his tone low with awe. "H. P. Lovecraft actually placed his head on this pillow and slept." He inhaled and caught a faint musty odor that reminded him of his office space in the basement. It almost made him dizzy. "Think of the *dreams* it must contain."

He smiled and glanced at the store owner, who appeared to be totally underwhelmed.

"The *inspiration.*"

"Yeah, whatever," the store owner said as he shifted the toothpick in his mouth from one side to the other. "What yah got there?"

His hands were hooked like the claws of a bird of prey as he reached for the laptop case slung over Martin's shoulder. Barely aware of what he was doing, Martin let go of the pillow with one hand and dropped his shoulder so the store owner could take the bag.

"Laptop, huh?" the man said, sounding vaguely interested. "Not sure how much something like this is worth. Don't get much demand for one of these in this neighborhood, yah know?"

Martin was barely paying attention to him as he gazed at the pillow in his hand. Merely touching it sent a shiver racing through him, and he knew—without any doubt—that he *had* to own this pillow.

"Even trade?" the store owner asked.

Martin found himself nodding his agreement without consciously thinking about it. He convinced himself that he didn't really *need* the laptop. It had been a luxury expense, and Alice was right; they really couldn't afford it. If he planned to keep writing, he would have to hook up his old desktop again. There must be someplace he could still buy floppy disks so he could back up his work.

"Deal," Martin said as he stuck out his hand and shook with the store owner.

"Whatever."

Moments later, Martin stepped out onto the sidewalk with the pillow tucked underneath his arm.

Just like *that*, the world looked different to him.

Maybe it was knowing what he was holding that changed his outlook, but already he was feeling inspired. He inhaled deeply, smelling the damp, rich scent of the freshly washed city. As he walked down the street, he watched with mild amusement as sunlight glanced off the soaped-over windows and shone in brilliant beams that reflected from puddles in the street. He watched a stray cat as it scrambled over a rusted chain-link fence and imagined the dark, dank places an animal like that would have to lurk in order to survive. He even smiled and nodded a greeting to the derelicts who asked him for any spare change.

"Grist for the mill," Martin whispered to himself as he started up the street, back to his house. "It's all grist for the mill."

"Martin?"

The sharp note in Alice's voice made Martin cringe, and he almost dropped the pillow—Lovecraft's pillow—which he had just slipped into his own pillowcase. He and Alice used contrasting colors for their bedsheets and pillowcases. The bottom sheet and Alice's pillowcase were white, and the top sheet and Martin's pillowcase were black. When they had first started doing this mix-and-match with their bed linens, Martin had been amused by the unorthodox aspect of it; but over the years—as he and Alice drifted further and further apart emotionally—he had come to see this as painfully symbolic of their relationship.

Moving quickly, Martin put the pillow back on his side of the bed, smoothed the bedspread over it, and turned around at the same moment Alice appeared in the bedroom doorway.

"I thought I heard you come in," she said, placing her hands on her hips and all but glaring at him. "How much did you get for the laptop?"

Martin swallowed with difficulty and, lowering his gaze, said, "The—uhh, the pawnshop was closed."

He almost choked on the lie. When he realized he was staring at the pillow on his side of the bed, he quickly shifted his gaze away from it, but he was positive Alice knew he was up to something. The muscles in the back of his neck and shoulders tensed as he waited for the inevitable question, but it never came. His wife shifted her weight from one foot to the other and crossed her arms over her chest.

"What are you waiting for?" she said. "Dinner first, and then you've *gotta* pay the bills."

Her voice had a high, reedy tone that made him all but shiver, but he was grateful she hadn't noticed or said anything about the pillow. He could imagine how much she would rip into him if she knew all he'd gotten for his laptop was a pillow.

Yeah, he thought with a thrill, *but what a pillow!*

Already, he couldn't wait for dinner to be over, the bills to be paid, and the night to come so he could go to bed as early as he could without making Alice suspicious. But dinner and cleaning up afterward took longer than usual because for some reason Alice decided to be chatty tonight, talking to him about everything that had happened to her today at the Dunkin' Donuts where she worked. When Martin finally went down to the cellar to pay the bills, it took him more than an hour to hook up his old computer. Other than a ridiculously long start-up, he thought it would be all right.

When he came upstairs and settled down at the dining-room table to pay the bills, he noticed in the stack of envelopes the rejection letter he'd gotten from *Cemetery Dance*. This was his eighth rejection since January. A deep, aching sadness filled him as he unfolded the letter and read it over a few times, trying to let it sink in.

Maybe Alice is right, he thought. *Maybe I should give it up.* But a tiny voice in the back of his mind was telling him *not* to quit. Not yet. The editor had included a handwritten note that was really encouraging, and—more importantly—Martin knew he had to sleep a few nights with Lovecraft's pillow to see what might happen. Then and only then, if he finally accepted that he was delusional about ever beating the odds and getting published, would he quit trying to write.

"Make sure you—" Alice shouted, but when she turned the corner and saw Martin at the dining room table, she lowered her voice. "—turn out the lights!"

From behind the stack of bills, Martin looked up at her, surprised to see that she had already changed into her nightgown.

"You're going to bed?"

"I'm exhausted," Alice said, scowling angrily. "I pulled another double shift today. I thought you'd be done with that by now."

"The—uhh—dishes took a little longer than I thought they would, and I—"

"—was downstairs, writing."

Martin cowered, wishing she would stop trying to second-guess him all the time.

"I was hooking up the old computer to see if it still works," he said.

"And does it?" Alice asked, sounding as if she really couldn't care one way or the other.

Martin shrugged. "I'll make do," he said in a soft voice as he opened the checkbook. He couldn't help but shake his head when he saw the balance in their account. There was no way he'd be able to pay everything this week or next. He listened to the tread of Alice's feet as she went upstairs, noticing that she turned out the hall light on her way. It didn't matter. He wouldn't be going up for a while yet. If he wasn't so excited about finding out what dreams and inspiration he would get sleeping on Lovecraft's pillow, he might have stayed up, watching *Letterman* and *The Late, Late Show* in order to avoid slipping into bed with . . . *her.*

But tonight . . .

"What dreams may come," he muttered when, after finishing paying the bills, he made his way up the stairs.

The instant he walked into the bedroom and saw what had happened, Martin felt a shock of utter disappointment. Then a spike of anger filled him as he approached the bed and saw that Alice really had swapped pillows with him. She had *his* pillow—*Lovecraft's* pillow—and was already sound asleep, lying on her right side with her back to him. Her arm was tucked underneath so the soft pillow cradled her head.

"For crying out—" Martin whispered, but then he cut himself off when Alice stirred in her sleep, rolling over so she was flat on her back. Her breathing was deep and watery sounding.

Martin stood where he was in the darkened bedroom for several minutes, staring at her and wondering how he was going to get

Lovecraft's pillow away from her. Leaning over the bed, he moved closer to her, looking for a way to get his pillow back. Alice's deep, ragged breathing was the only sound in the room, but inside his head, Martin could hear the hard, steady rush of blood.

What was he going to do?

No matter what, he couldn't face the firestorm if he woke her up while trying to take his pillow back. Her pillow—the white one—had dropped onto the floor beside the bed. Finally, realizing he had to give it up, Martin heaved a heavy sigh, picked up Alice's pillow, and placed it on his side of the bed. Then he went to the bathroom and brushed his teeth before retiring. When he turned off the light, a pale blue cast of moonlight filled the room. With one last, disappointed look at Lovecraft's pillow, he settled down into bed.

But the instant his weight sank onto the mattress, Alice stirred.

"Beyond the wall . . . Y'golonac sleeps."

In the moonlit darkness, her voice sounded much deeper than usual, and there was a weird distortion to it that sent chills through Martin. He rolled over in bed and, leaning over his wife, brought his face close to her. Still sound asleep, she smacked her lips and then started tossing her head from side to side.

"The tattered, eyeless ones serve him . . ." she said in a voice that modulated up and down with an odd echo. "Crawling on his body, awaiting the time he can return. Waiting . . . waiting . . ."

The whole time she was muttering, Martin kept drawing his face closer and closer to her, waiting for an opportunity when she rolled her head to one side and he could snatch the pillow out from under her.

Alice started whispering now, words that made absolutely no sense to Martin but which chilled him nonetheless. Her moaning grew louder. As she tossed her head furiously, the pillow under it started to make strange sucking sounds. At the moment Martin was steeling himself to grab the pillow, Alice's eyes shot open, and with a sharp intake of breath, she sat bolt upright in bed. Before Martin could react, she let out the most blood-curdling scream he had ever heard.

It was several hours later, and Martin was pacing back and forth in the hospital hallway when the resident who was on duty that night walked up to him. The nametag on his pale green surgical shirt read DR. BROWN. He was a tall man with thinning dark hair and glasses so thick they distorted his eyes, making him look like he was in a state of perpetual surprise.

Martin had stopped pacing right outside the door to the locked room where Alice was being kept. Before Dr. Brown could say a word, Alice, her arms bound in a straitjacket, suddenly lurched into sight in the doorway and slammed herself against the wire-reinforced window so hard the door rattled, and the sound echoed like a cannon shot in the long hallway.

Dr. Brown lowered his head sympathetically and, placing one hand on Martin's shoulder, directed him away from the window. Alice's long, dark hair was disheveled, and her bloodshot eyes were open so wide the whites showed all around her pupils. Flecks of thick yellow mucus covered her trembling lower lip, and the glass muffled her shouting as they walked away. Just before they turned the corner, Martin glanced back and saw her staring after them. When she started screaming, he looked away.

"I'm sorry you have to see this," Dr. Brown said. He was holding a clipboard with a medical chart, and he glanced down at it.

"Do you have any idea what's wrong with her?" Martin asked. His voice caught in his throat, and he had to clench his hands into fists to stop them from shaking.

"At this point," Dr. Brown said, "all we know for sure is that she's had a complete mental breakdown. There were no warning signs?"

Martin considered for a moment and then shook his head.

"No history of mental illness in the family?"

"None that I'm aware of," Martin said. He had to stop himself from adding *Unless being a total bitch, twenty-four seven, is a sign of mental illness.*

"Is she on any medications?"

"Just one for high blood pressure."

"No other prescription drugs or, perhaps, was she taking any illicit drugs?"

"No. Of course not," Martin said, biting his lower lip and shaking his head.

Clearly baffled, Dr. Brown looked at the ceiling for a moment or two before saying, "Well, we'll have to keep her here so we can conduct a complete battery of tests. For now, though, it's challenge enough keeping her sedated."

Even though they had rounded the corner at the end of the hall, Martin could still feel Alice's insane stare on his back, and he cringed inwardly, knowing or at least suspecting he knew exactly what had caused this. And the saddest thing about it—what might even be proof that he himself was sick—was that Martin knew it was all grist for the mill, and that he had what he wanted: inspiration for one hell of a story.

"I'm very sorry, Mr. Hale," Dr. Brown said. "I wish I could be more hopeful."

The bells above the pawnshop door jingled when Martin swung the door open and entered. The store owner was leaning against the counter, resting on both elbows as he flipped through the pages of a girlie magazine. If the man hadn't been wearing a different shirt from the previous day, Martin might have suspected he had slipped back in time.

Another cool idea for a story, he thought as he walked up to the counter and held out the blue-and-white-striped pillow.

"I need to trade this back for my laptop. Now," he said in as firm a voice as he could muster.

The store owner regarded him in silence for a few seconds as he took a deep breath and shifted the toothpick from one corner of his mouth to the other.

"Gonna cost yah an extra fifty bucks," he finally said.

Martin sighed as he fished his wallet out of his back pocket and opened it. After buying lunch, all he had left was two $20 bills, which he took out and held up to the man.

"Will forty do?" he asked, trying to keep the pleading note out of his voice. "It's all I got until I sell a story."

The store owner drew back and scowled as if he didn't like the deal, but Martin suspected he was more than happy to make forty bucks for doing nothing.

"You said you don't have much demand for laptops."

"Or old pillows," he said with a faint sneer, but that didn't stop him from taking the $40 and Lovecraft's pillow from Martin.

He moved over to the window display and put the pillow right back where Martin had first seen it. He put the sign in place, then handed Martin his laptop without another word.

Satisfied, Martin left the pawnshop, but as the bells jingled and the door swung shut behind him, he hesitated on the sidewalk and stared at the pillow in the window display. The store owner was still standing in the doorway, and for a moment their eyes met and locked.

I should tell him what that pillow does to people, Martin thought.

He started to move back toward the door, but before he opened it, he sighed and, shaking his head, turned and left.

Maybe what happened had nothing to do with Lovecraft's pillow, he told himself as he started back toward home.

Maybe Alice had been on the road to a mental break for a long time now . . .

Maybe all the money pressures and their deteriorating relationship had finally gotten the better of her and she had finally snapped . . .

Maybe she would have had a breakdown whether or not she had taken his pillow from him last night.

Maybe the whole thing was all in his imagination . . .

But now more than ever Martin was confident that he had what a writer really needed to succeed. He had imagination—and inspiration—and with or without Alice in his life, he had a lot of perseverance.

As soon as he got back to the house, he started moving his office up from the basement and into the living room. It took him most of the afternoon to get things set up the way he wanted them, with his writing desk and bookcases in front of the window. The view outside wasn't much—a small, weed-choked front yard that faced another modest home like his across the street.

But there was sunlight and fresh air swirling in through the opened window, and he had his laptop back. He was positive now that he had all the inspiration he needed to write a story that the editors at *Cemetery Dance* would be foolish to reject.

And the title?

That was the easiest part.

The title was "Lovecraft's Pillow."

One Twenty-Eight,
Give or Take

"LOOK AT THIS, WOULD YOU? IT'S AN INVITE TO MY TENTH high school reunion."

"You going?"

"I don't want to but my wife is crazy for it. She says she wants to find out who I was before we met."

"Do you have anything to worry about?"

"Sure. She'll find out what a geek I was and won't believe I'm really me. What about you guys? Ever go to one of these?"

"I do. To the big ones, anyway. My thirtieth is this year. But Bruce doesn't. Do you, Bruce?"

"Nope. Not anymore."

"What does that mean?"

"Means he used to."

"That's right. And now I don't."

"Ask him why."

"Okay. Why?"

"Because of a patient I once had."

"Come on, Bruce, tell him the whole story."

"Oh, all right. This happened about ten, maybe eleven years ago. I had this patient. And the first time I saw him, he was only interested in telling me about this dream he'd had the night before our first appointment. He wanted to skip over all the usual preliminary stuff. He said that could come later. The important thing was this dream he'd had."

"Which was?"

"That he had gone to his twentieth high school reunion."

"Come on. You're pulling my leg."

"No, he's not. Listen."

"Now, you have to understand that this was a guy who had no business being at his high school reunion. I mean, high school reunions are for the popular people, right? Football players and cheerleaders. Like that, you know? Not like this guy. He was horribly bullied all four years. He was small, so they used to stuff him in trash cans and roll him down this big hill at the back of campus. He wore glasses, so they used to take those away from him and hide them. He wore braces, so they used to call him every name in the book. Every morning before class, he would open his locker and they would slam it shut so he would have to go through the whole combination again. And they would do this until he cried. Girls were completely out of the question. Of course he had crushes on all of them. He even wrote an anonymous love letter to the one he really liked. But get this, he put his return address on the envelope because he thought the post office wouldn't deliver it otherwise. So of course this girl's friends knew that he wrote the letter. They looked his name up in the phone book. They saw the return address matched this love letter and the next day at school, they let him have it. So like I said, this guy has no reason to go to his high school reunion. Except the one that guys like him do have."

"Which is?"

"Revenge, of course. Think about it. That's all this guy has got. And he tells me so in our first meeting. He says this is why the dream is so important. And he tells me all this stuff I just told you because he wants to put it in context for me. He tells me that even when he was in high school, he used to dream about becoming world famous so he could come to his five-year reunion and pull up in a black stretch limo and get out holding the hand of a model or something. And he would picture all these bullies suddenly falling down at his feet and begging his forgiveness and wanting to be his friend and he would imagine himself saying 'No.'"

"How long ago was this?"

"Hold on. Let him finish. Go ahead, Bruce."

"So this guy fantasizes about this kind of stuff all the time. He gets out of high school, finally. Goes to college. Dedicates himself to figuring out how to become world famous so he can have this elaborate revenge, but it isn't quite that easy, right? The five-year reunion arrives and this guy isn't any closer to achieving his goal. And he gets angrier. He blames all the people at his high school for his failings. He starts to think that maybe some of them have followed him and somehow gotten jobs at the college and they're making the professors give him bad grades. And pretty soon, his revenge fantasies aren't only about showing up in a black stretch limo, they're about somehow becoming so famous that he actually refuses to even go to his reunion. And he imagines himself at home in his mansion watching the news reports about his reunion and his not showing up. And now the bullies are all crying. And the girls are wishing he would show just so they could throw themselves at him. And this one girl he wrote the love letter to is holding the letter and telling the reporter that she always loved him. But, unfortunately, his ten-year reunion arrives and he's still no closer to becoming famous. He's working as a stock broker and he's got a pretty good job. But he's not married because he's spending so much time working on his goal, everything else is taking a back seat. So finally, he starts to accept the fact that it's not going to happen the way he wants it to. And that's when he has this dream. This 'prophetic' dream, he calls it."

"And this is the one he tells you about during your first meeting?"

"Exactly. And the dream is simple. He goes to his twentieth high school reunion and he gives them all a batch of Jonestown punch."

"What's that?"

"He's too young to remember, Bruce."

"Are you kidding me?"

"Look at his face."

"Okay. Jonestown punch is poison Kool-Aid. You ever hear of Jim Jones? People's Temple? Gave everybody poison to drink."

"And that's this guy's dream?"

"Yes. But he says to me that I shouldn't be worried. He tells me that he understands absolutely such a thing would, of course, be terribly wrong. Against the law and all that. But he wants me to know that he has had this dream, and what do I think?"

"Did you call the cops?"

"No."

"No?"

"No. I told him our time was up and I would see him the next week and we could pick up where we left off."

"You're kidding me."

"No."

"So what happened?"

"So he comes in the next week. And he tells me he wants to skip all the preliminary stuff. That can come later, he says. What he's really anxious to do is tell me this dream he had."

"About his twentieth high school reunion."

"Exactly. Goes through the whole story again. Like I've never heard it before. Like he's never told it before. And he's absolutely convinced it's only a dream."

"What do you mean?"

"Do you remember Hugh Derrickson?"

"No way."

"That's him. One hundred twenty-eight people. Give or take a few. I think one or two of them survived. Seems like I saw one of them on *Oprah* last month or something. Wrote a book about it."

"And he thought it was a dream?"

"Oh, it was. For ten years, anyway. Once he'd actually done it, well . . . he did the only thing he could do. He kept on believing that it was only a dream. Kept telling himself that he understood absolutely how terribly wrong it would be if he actually did anything like that."

"Oh my God."

"So you can see why Bruce is kind of put off by the whole reunion thing, right?"

"No kidding."

"So what are you going to tell your wife?"

"About what?"

"About going to your reunion."

"What do you think?"

The
Barn

THE BARN WAS DIFFERENT TODAY. IMPOSSIBLE, OF COURSE, that a barn could change overnight. Yet somehow it had. It seemed bigger than before. Out of place, too. Before today, the barn had always seemed like a natural part of the landscape, as if it belonged right where it was, there between the house and the stand of oak trees. The bright red walls and white trim had looked as natural a feature of the terrain as the rope swing over the river at Jacob's Point or the well behind Carl's Gas-N-Go. Yes, they were man-made things, but they *belonged*. Like the barn. Only not today. Today the barn looked out of place. Like a fly on a vanilla ice cream cone. Like the flayed corpse of some prehistoric creature, all red muscle and white bone gleaming in the hot sun. Someone would have to do something about it, of course. Cover it up. Take it away. Someone would have to call Doc Otter to come over from Preston. The sheriff would have to be there, too. One of them would ask to use the phone to call Murray from the funeral parlor. And what good would it do? Not a spot. A body of that size could never be moved, not even with one of those mobile-home haulers. No. Only one way to get rid of it. They would have to burn it right there. The stench and smoke would both be blinding, no doubt. Then it would be gone, and after a few days, the feeling would pass. The sting would dull to a throb and only the memory of the pain would stay behind. Then the barn would look like it belonged again. And this moment, too, would be nothing but a memory.

Not now, though. Now a little breeze shifted and blew the coppery scent of blood past his face. He rubbed his nose and turned away, the same as he did when he brought home a bag of pheasant. Inside the house, the phone rang, and he started for the door, glad for the interruption. He would deal with the barn later.

"Yello," he said.

"Jeb?" It was Murray, from the funeral parlor. "Is that you?"

"Course it's me," Jeb said. "Who else would be answering the phone in my house?"

"Don't sound like yourself."

Jeb shook his head. People always said dumb things like that. Didn't make any sense. Like always answering "I'm fine" when someone asked "How are you?" Even if you weren't. He'd heard Martha do it countless times in their twenty-five years together.

"Jeb?" Murray said, quieter than before. "You still there?"

"Course I'm still here. Where else would I go? What do you want?"

"I'm calling about the arrangements."

Jeb turned away from the empty spot on the wall, the place where Matt's photo had been. "Arrangements," he muttered. Another one of those dumb things people said to cover up what they really meant. Like "passed away" when they meant a body had died.

"That's right," Murray said.

For a moment, Jeb wondered if Doc Otter and the sheriff had already been there. Had he called them about the barn? Had he already forgotten their coming and going? Then he remembered. Of course they had been there. Not for the barn, though. "I told you before," Jeb said, "pick out whatever you think is best. I don't care what it costs. I know you'll do me right and not take advantage. Besides, the coffin'll only be half normal size, so we ought to be able to get one twice as fancy for the same price as a plain big one, ain't that right? I know Martha wants a fancy one." And there it was again. Another one of those stupid things people do. Build a beautiful coffin, line it with silk, paint it pretty, then put it in a hole in the ground to rot along with the putrid flesh inside. He didn't really think Martha was stupid like most people, just that she went along with everyone a little more often than she ought to.

"Yes," Murray said, "you did tell me that before. I'm calling to let you know the service has been scheduled for tomorrow at two o'clock."

"Oh," Jeb said. "Okay. Tomorrow at two o'clock."

"I'll send a car to pick you and Martha up at one thirty, okay?"

"A car? How much is that going to cost?"

"It's included, Jeb. We find it best if people don't drive themselves."

"Afraid their grief'll make them crash into someone, are you?"

"Something like that."

"Is that all?"

"How's Martha holding up?"

"Fine, Murray. Just like me." Jeb hung up the phone without saying goodbye and suddenly realized he'd gone and done one of the dumb things himself. He chuckled once, bitterly, then decided he had better clean the hay baler.

The sheriff had offered to finish the job, after Doc Otter and Murray had picked Matthew's body out of the rollers and put the pieces into the black plastic bags they had brought with them. Jeb had refused. He believed what his father had told him: a man cleans up his own messes.

"But this is different," the sheriff had said. "A father shouldn't have to do this."

"The world don't work on shoulds," Jeb had said, and he had waited for them to leave.

Jeb stopped behind the house to fill a bucket with water and pluck a rag down from the laundry line. Only there were no rags on the laundry line, just three of Martha's dresses, a pair of his coveralls, and some of Matthew's t-shirts. "Rags now," he said as he grabbed one of the shirts off the line, dropped it in the bucket, and continued to the baler.

He set the bucket down in the dirt and stared at the rollers. The blood didn't look like blood. Then he realized it wasn't blood at all, but rust. The sheriff had gone and cleaned it for him, in spite of what Jeb had said.

Jeb was disappointed. He had felt that cleaning his boy's blood off those rollers would help him somehow. That the act of cleaning would dull the sting he was feeling inside. And now that chance was gone. The sheriff had taken it away from him. What could he do? Ask the sheriff to bring his boy's body back and run it through the baler again so he'd have something to clean? Of course not. The sheriff would think he'd gone crazy. "Already thinks I've gone crazy," Jeb said out loud, then he realized he was talking to himself, just like a crazy person.

He snatched up the bucket and swung it in an angry arc over his head, slamming it down onto the rollers. The water spilled into the dirt at his feet, and he slipped in the mud as the bucket bounced out of his hand. He reached for something to hold on to and caught a bolt that snicked the web between his thumb and index finger. He sat down hard, balled his hand into a fist, and watched the blood run down his wrist. Without hesitation, he held his hand over the rollers and waited for a few drops to fall onto the rusted yellow metal. Then he got to his feet, picked Matthew's shirt out of the fallen bucket, and wiped the blood away. It wasn't the same, but it would have to do.

Jeb dropped the shirt on the ground and started toward the house. At the edge of the field, he realized what a mess he was leaving behind, and the irony tasted bitter in his mouth. "I'll clean it up later," he muttered as he went inside to find a Band-Aid.

He thought about lunch, then saw it was already 2:30. He thought about dealing with the barn again, but decided he was too tired to do anything except find the couch and close his eyes.

He woke up after dark and nearly knocked the lamp over trying to turn it on. He thought for a moment that he heard Matthew calling his name. No. Not anymore. Matt hadn't had nightmares since he'd been very young. He was twelve now. A teenager next year. Driving soon. High school. Then college. A job in the city. Wife. More kids than just one. A family ought to have more kids than just one. Then in case something terrible happens, the family can take care of each other.

Jeb suddenly realized he was crying, and he hit his fist on the coffee table hard enough to open the cut in his hand and knock the water glass over. "Another mess to clean up," he said, standing. If he let things keep going this way, he would soon be surrounded by messes. His life would turn into one big mess and he wouldn't have time to clean it all up.

He wiped the tears from his stubble-covered cheeks, then wiped his hand on his coveralls and nodded. He should start now. "Always start with the biggest job," he remembered his father telling him. "Everything else comes easy after that."

In Jeb's case, that meant the barn. He bowed his head and went outside.

As it had that morning, the barn still looked out of place. The full moon shining down turned the bones ash gray. The red muscle, so bright in the sun earlier, now looked purple and black, like a bruise. He moved toward it slowly. The breeze shifted again, only this time it wasn't the coppery smell of blood he caught but the sweet smell of rot.

He stood in front of the barn's gaping black maw and stared into the darkness, thinking about how many times he had told Matthew not to play on the hay baler. Like everything else he had told him.

Like brush your teeth and comb your hair and do your homework and sit up straight and chew with your mouth closed and say "Please" and "Thank you" and say your prayers and "DON'T PLAY ON THE HAY BALER!"

Far as Jeb knew, he had said all those other things enough times for Matthew to understand. He'd even told him how a real man cleans up his messes, just like *his* father had told *him*. And Matthew had always cleaned up his messes. But maybe Jeb hadn't told his boy not to play on the hay baler enough times. Maybe if he had said it just once more, it would have sunk in deep enough for him to listen. Maybe if he had told him just once more, Matthew wouldn't have played on the hay baler and he would still be there, sleeping upstairs in his room.

Course, Martha would still be alive, too. She wouldn't have hanged herself from the winch rope off the loft inside the barn. Jeb wouldn't have ever called Doc Otter or the sheriff or Murray. He wouldn't be getting in a car tomorrow at 1:30 to go to his son's funeral. He wouldn't be opening this can of gasoline to pour around the barn because it wouldn't look out of place.

Jeb shook the can empty and tossed it aside. He reached into his pocket and found the book of matches he always kept with him. That was all he wanted, you know—for the barn to look like it belonged where it was, not like some giant animal corpse he was going to have to burn to get rid of now.

Jeb struck one match, used it to set the whole book on fire, then crouched down and dropped it in a puddle of gasoline. The flames spread quickly along the barn's front. The red-and-white paint blistered and bubbled and popped as the fire turned it black and chewed into the wood underneath. He and Matthew had painted it last summer. Martha had brought them lunch and lemonade every day for a week. And in the evening, they had sat on the porch and watched the sun go down. The barn had looked right then. Yes, sir. The barn had looked right, then.

Jeb stepped through the open door. The fire was coming around the corners now and the inside was alive with jumping shadows. He glanced up at Martha overhead and saw her wink at him. Then he realized that the flies had already gotten to her and it was the maggots crawling around, not a wink. Had it already been three days?

Jeb used a pitchfork to dig himself a flat space in the pile of hay under the loft, then crawled in and rolled over on his side. He could hear the fire behind him, getting closer. Then he could feel it. Then he could see it, even with his eyes shut.

Death Wears
a Smile

You who see my smiling face
And my gentle disposition
Could never imagine the thoughts so base
Hidden as the secrets of a magician

You who see my joyful gait
And say, "Now there's a happy one"
Could never know the blackest hate
That fuels the deeds I've done

You who hear my jolly laughter
And say you like my humor
Could never see the shadowy rafter
Where lives the noose of my tumor

You who think you know who I am
Know not the slightest shred
Until your very soul I damn
When I strike you down and dead

Death is at peace, my friend
For he has but one job to do—
That is to bring on the end
Not asking when, but only who

Like him I wear but a smile
For what better way to conceal
That my veins course with the black bile
Of desire for your soul to steal

So the next time you meet me
And shake my cold hand
Remember this whispered secret and see
Into my eyes—into that wasteland

You never know when I'll strike
But then, that's half the fun
Of playing the game until
All is said and done

The Book
Smeller

Eugene takes the book from the shelf and turns it over in his hands. His eyebrows lift in hopeful expectation as he places his right thumb on the front cover and casts a casual glance over his left shoulder. Once he is sure no one is watching, he lifts the book to his nose, closes his eyes, and flips through the pages rapidly, inhaling their smell as deeply as he can.

Disappointment clouds his face as he sourly regards the book one last time before roughly shoving it back onto the shelf. "Close," he whispers, "very close indeed. But still, not exactly right. A seven, to be sure, but not an eight. Maybe the next one. Maybe the next one."

Some people collect books by author or genre, some by cover art or age, some by condition or rarity. Not Eugene Escott. That's because Eugene is a book smeller. And for the book smeller, there is nothing quite as perfect as the smell of a used paperback. Hardcovers simply don't smell the same. New paperbacks are okay (some are better than others, for sure), but, like wine, they aren't as good as an older book, properly aged on a wooden shelf in the dry corner of a secondhand shop.

Eugene does not remember when he first noticed that he liked books for their smell more than anything else. He always enjoyed

reading when he was a child, but once he started his collection in
earnest more than ten years ago, he stopped reading altogether.

In the beginning, Eugene just set aside the books he thought
smelled better. Each night, he took a few with his cup of tea and sat
up in bed, watching TV and smelling their pages over and over again.
Eventually, he realized that some books smelled markedly better
than others, and he began to establish a rating system.

One, he decided, was the least favorable smell; seven, the most
favorable. Ah, sevens. How often he had fallen asleep with a seven
tented on his face. After awakening one morning to discover that he
had broken a seven in half, Eugene had decided he needed to protect
his collection better. And although he had enough money to hire the
job out, because Eugene didn't want to explain the curious purpose of
the room in his attic, he built it himself.

Eugene wasn't ashamed of his collection, not at all. He was, in
fact, quite proud of it. He just had a feeling people wouldn't understand him. And he already had enough of that problem, thank you
very much. He didn't want to make things worse by running around,
waving books at people, saying "Smell this. Smell this." He was angry
that he couldn't, of course. People spent their lives sniffing wine and
tasting coffee beans, why shouldn't he be able to smell his books?

Once, about five years ago, Eugene had considered founding a
book-smelling society. He was sure there were others like him out
there; he just needed to find them. He was so sure, in fact, that he
put an ad in the personals section of the city weekly. The first few
responses were scathing diatribes laden with words such as "freak"
and "weirdo" and "loser." It amazed him that people actually had time
to write such negative things. Wouldn't they rather spend their lives
like he did, pursuing things that made them happy?

When he received an e-mail from someone named Ella asking
for a meeting at the south branch of the city library on Monday
afternoon, Eugene was too excited to do anything except call in sick

to work and take the number 29 bus to First and Main. When he arrived, he found the library closed. Of course it was closed. It was Monday afternoon. And right when he thought Ella's elaborate joke was over, he turned around to find three frat boys with crewcuts and eyes filled with cold hate.

"Are you the freak who took out the ad looking for book smellers?" one of them asked.

"Of course he is," said another. "He's here, isn't he?"

"All right then," the third one said, "smell this."

He saw only blurs as they each lifted books and closed in. The first blow hit him on the side of the head and knocked his glasses off. The second hit him in the stomach; the third, across the shins. Eugene dropped to the ground and crawled forward. When he reached the steps, he fell completely flat, and two of the boys tripped over him, striking the pavement hard enough to scrape their hands and draw blood. This only seemed to enrage them more, but before they could renew their attack, a car horn honked and they fled. Eugene looked up and saw his savior was an old woman in a station wagon stopped next to the book-return kiosk. "Are you okay?" she called, but he was too humiliated to answer. He didn't even stop to find his glasses.

After that day, Eugene knew he had to keep his collection completely private. He never even told his mother.

Ironically, only after the incident at the library had Eugene really thrown himself into his collection. In the five years since, he had amassed more than three thousand books, all charted and shelved according to the classification system he invented. He no longer brings the books out of their place in the attic. In fact, he spends more time collecting than he does smelling.

About a month ago, however, Eugene began to wonder if there couldn't, in fact, be an eight: a book whose smell is so perfect that it exceeds every other book in his collection. Initially, Eugene tried to dismiss the thought, but like a person told not to think about purple squirrels, he soon became obsessed, first with the possibility that an eight could exist, then with actually finding one.

After a week of looking, Eugene was suddenly struck with the notion that he might already have an eight, and he hurried home to sniff his way through his collection again. He only had a dozen sevens, but to his horror, he discovered that one of them now smelled suspiciously like a six. Eugene tried to convince himself that he had simply made a mistake with the first classification. But even before he had cleared a new spot on the six shelf, he realized the truth: the book had lost some of its smell. He had never considered the possibility that, like wine, books might also turn to vinegar. This meant that his eleven sevens would soon all be sixes. And that his sixes would be fives and his fives, fours. Eugene stumbled backwards from the shelves under the weight of this revelation. Once he had found the strength to stand again, he left the attic, went down into the kitchen, and brewed himself a strong cup of tea.

"Get hold of yourself, Eugene," he whispered. "Maybe it's only that one book." Yes. Maybe it was only that one book. And to prove it to himself, he hurried back upstairs and started through his entire collection from the bottom up.

He looked up each book's rating, then pulled it from the shelf and smelled it. Soon, however, he realized that he was likely being influenced by knowing the rating before he smelled the book. He switched then, pulling a book and smelling it, then deciding on a rating, and only then checking it against what he had already assigned to the title. The first few matched, and he began to feel some relief. Until he discovered another book that was different from the original classification he had assigned to it. Only this time, the book had gained a level. What had been a one, he now rated a two. At first, this filled Eugene with joy. *Of course,* he thought. *It takes time for books to acquire their more favorable odors.* And when he checked the date of the first classification, he saw that it was two years ago. In two years, the book had gained one full level. This meant that some of the books in his collection were therefore actually improving. "But," he muttered. That meant that he might, in fact, have let some books he had rated as fives or sixes attain the scent of sevens only to let them fade back to fives or fours—or worse. Eugene didn't even want to consider the possibility that somewhere in his collection a seven had become an eight and then become a seven again.

Eugene couldn't sleep at all that night. The next morning, he called in sick and began completely reclassifying his collection. The process took a week, and when he was finished, he took the box of zeroes to Earl at the Paperback Reader and accepted a trade slip in exchange. He didn't feel right about the transaction. As far as he was concerned, a box of zeroes belonged in the trash, but Earl seemed enthusiastic about a number of the titles. A shame he didn't care about the smell the way Eugene did. With that finished, Eugene resumed his search.

He knew now that time was of the essence. An eight—if he could find one—would never remain in such a state of perfection. Surely, it would only last for a short period of time. Not a year. A few months, perhaps. Maybe even a few weeks. Maybe even only a few days. This lent a greater urgency to Eugene's quest, and he called in sick every day. When he hadn't been to work for nearly a month, he returned home one night to find a message from his boss telling him he had been fired.

"Good," Eugene said to his bedroom walls. In fact, a sudden smile sprang to life on his unshaven face as he realized that his dream had come true. He was a full-time book smeller now.

Eugene pulls another book from the shelf and turns it over in his hands. His eyebrows lift in hopeful expectation as he places his right thumb on the front cover and casts a casual glance over his left shoulder. Once he is sure no one is watching, he lifts the book to his nose, closes his eyes, and flips through the pages rapidly, inhaling their smell as deeply as he can.

Disappointment again clouds his face as he sourly regards the book one last time before roughly shoving it back onto the shelf. "Close," he whispers, "very close indeed. But still, not exactly right. A seven, to be sure, but not an eight. Maybe the next one. Maybe the next one."

Sleepless

THE GLOWING RED NUMBERS STARE THROUGH THE DARK AT you like an accusation—12:37—yet still you cannot sleep. This was what you told your wife two hours ago, that you were not tired, you would stay up to read. But that didn't work. You tried a glass of wine, usually a sure way to knock you out, but not tonight. Tonight it was as if you'd had coffee.

You turn away from the clock and stare at the foot of your bed, where your cat sleeps soundly, his legs and whiskers twitching in a dream. You envy him his peace and wonder why yours won't come. When you face the clock again (1:12), you realize that even if you get to sleep now it will be less than five hours before you have to get up again.

You stare at the ceiling, still not tired. You close your eyes, but your mind is wide awake, as busy with thoughts as a hive with bees seeking their queen. You roll onto your side, then onto your stomach, trying to relax, but your limbs are coiled wire—as cold, as tight. Next to you, your wife breathes heavily and mumbles dream nonsense. You roll over and meet the clock's glowing face again. 2:17 now. You pretend your eyes are heavy, but after only a few moments, they snap open again, not tricked.

A car drives through the alley behind your bedroom, and its

headlights cut across the ceiling like a flash of lightning. You hear the distant rattle of a transient's shopping cart come and go. A cat fight. A gunshot. A train whistle. Shouting voices. The city night is alive with other people not asleep. Surely that is their choice. Not like you. Not *unable* to sleep.

At 3:24, you grow worried. You think first about how tired you'll be, how it might affect your work. The worries spin in your head, whirl-pooling into concerns about your health. You've never had insomnia before. Is something wrong with you?

At 5:30, the alarm buzzes and you get out of bed. You feel strange, dazed, like the last time you had the flu. You remember how you came and went in sleep all through the day. When you awakened at dusk, you mistook it for dawn. That is how you feel now.

In the shower, you try to wash away your worries, but they will not go. At least you're not tired. You drink coffee anyway and read the morning paper, hoping the routine will ease your mind. It doesn't. You awaken your wife at 6:02, then eat breakfast and leave to catch the train.

At the office, you lose yourself for minutes at a time while you concentrate on working, but then you remember you have not slept since yesterday and you worry again. At the end of the day, you tell yourself you will sleep tonight. All the way home, you visualize your-self sleeping. After dinner, you have another glass of wine. While you watch television, you have another. Still, you are as wide awake as a child on Christmas morning. At 10:12, you follow your wife to bed. Within minutes, her rhythmic breathing fills the room, but you are still awake, staring at the ceiling, your worries double what they were the night before. The red glow of the clock leaks into the edge of your vision, like blood in water.

At 12:24, you get out of bed and quietly go to the bathroom. You open the medicine chest to search for sleeping pills, but find none. You get dressed and drive to the store.

Back home, you read the directions. No more than two. Not to be taken with alcohol. You swallow four, then chase them with a double scotch from the dusty bottle you find in the cupboard. You sit on the couch and watch TV and wait. At 1:44, you are still not sleepy. You are worried now, more than you have been yet. You consider taking more pills, but you don't want to kill yourself. You decide to call a doctor tomorrow, and you go back to bed again. But still you cannot sleep.

At 5:30, the alarm buzzes and again you get out of bed. Again you go into the shower. Again you eat breakfast. When you wake your wife this time, you consider telling her what is happening, but you don't. No need to worry her, too.

The doctor has an appointment available in the early afternoon. When you tell your boss that's where you're going, he asks if you're all right. You lie and say you are.

After you've talked to the doctor, you feel somewhat relieved. He finds it hard to believe, especially the part about the alcohol and sleeping pills. "Aren't you aware of the danger you put yourself in?" he asks. You nod sheepishly and ask him what might be wrong. He checks you over and tells you it's nothing physical. Maybe it's psychological. Perhaps you have some deep worry, something you're feeling guilty about. You nod and smile, but you know better. You aren't guilty of anything. Until this insomnia, you hadn't a worry in the world. He writes a prescription for sleeping pills and asks you to call him in two days.

On your way out of the pharmacy, you are so desperate you take two of the pills, hoping they will work. But somehow, you know they won't. They don't. On your way home, you take four more and stop off at the corner bar for two double scotches. Still you are not tired.

During dinner, your wife asks what's wrong. You want to tell her, but now you'll have to explain why you didn't after the first night. Better to let it go, you think. So you lie to her, saying work is more than you expected, that's all. She frowns and nods.

After dinner, you take six of the pills, your hands trembling with fear. Why won't they work? Why can't you sleep?

At 10:33, you and your wife go to bed. You dare yourself not to meet the clock's red eyes. But the more you think about it, the weaker you become. The clock taunts you, glowing brighter somehow. You squeeze your eyes shut but still see red. The longer you hold off looking at it, the more desperately you need to look, to know how long you've been able to go without looking at it. You open your eyes. 11:07. You roll away and find your wife sleeping soundly next to you. You feel hot tears at the back of your throat, but manage to stop them there.

At 11:39, you get up and go into the front room again. You are staring at the television when suddenly the black screen bends toward you. You blink and it falls flat again. Your heart races. You suddenly remember reading something about lack of sleep causing hallucinations. Your fear redoubles. You feel trapped. The walls of your apartment seem to close in on you like a giant's mouth. You need to get out. Quickly, you dress and hurry down to the street.

For three hours, you walk in circles downtown, five blocks this way, four blocks that way. Everywhere you see clocks: on banks, in stores. The minutes tease you with their slowness. To avoid the clocks, you look at the people. People whose job it is to stay awake: the clerks behind the counters at the mini-markets and the pornographic bookstores, the security guards. You think you should get a second job, perhaps even two more jobs, and for the first time in three days, you smile. Then you realize it's no joke.

Someone whispers in your ear and you turn quickly, startled, but the street corner is empty. You face forward again, in time to see a man in a black coat dart behind the tree next to you. Needles on your neck, you back away. You call out, telling whoever it is behind the tree to show himself. But there is no answer. You step forward carefully, bracing yourself. But when you round the tree, you find only shadows.

You hurry home. Every crack in the sidewalk yawns before you, so you must jump over them or fall in. At the corner a block from your building, you see someone watching you and suddenly feel foolish. Nothing but your mind playing tricks on you, that's all.

Upstairs, you are quietly slipping the key into the front door when you hear your wife inside, talking with someone. Anger replaces your fear. Who would she have over at this hour? But even as you open the door, you realize it is another trick. When you see only darkness, you close the door and slump onto the couch and let the tears come. Your cat awakens and looks at you, then yawns and goes back to sleep. You stare at the ceiling and beg God if He's out there to please let you sleep. For the first time, death seems like a pleasant alternative to this creeping madness, but you quickly blot the thought from your head and get undressed and go back to bed. Still you are not tired.

At 5:30, the alarm buzzes again. In the shower, you are sure you're going to suffocate. When your wife calls your name, you shut off the water and answer her, but the bathroom is empty, of course. Your wife is still in bed, sleeping peacefully.

At work, you call the doctor and tell him you still have not slept. You tell him about the hallucinations and he confirms what you suspected: such occurrences are the by-product of sleep deprivation. He refers you to a specialist at the hospital. You call him, but they have no appointments available until the following Monday. You tell them it's an emergency, but the man on the other end of the line can only tell you the doctor is gone and won't be back until Monday. You take the appointment, but you're sure you won't last until then. When you hang up, you tell yourself there's always the emergency room.

At home that night, you eat dinner and your wife gets ready to go out to a movie with friends. She tells you not to wait up for her. But she can't know what a cruel joke she has made. You smile wanly and watch her go.

The house is empty and silent. But not for you. For you, it is a madhouse. Everywhere, the sound of whispering voices. In every corner, a hunched man with a knife waits to spring at you, a hand on your shoulder, a tongue behind your ear, an insect burrowing under the pale flesh of your forearm. You bury your head in pillows, trying to blot it all out, but in your inner darkness, the hallucinations only redouble.

Frantic, barely able to, you go to the desk and find a pad of paper. You scratch out a note, begging your wife to forgive what you are about to do. Then you go into the bathroom and turn on the hot water. From the medicine chest, you take down a double-edged razor blade and tear off the cardboard wrapping. As the mirror clouds with steam, the last glimpse of yourself is your face covered with fire. You wrench your eyes shut and turn your head away. You turn one wrist up and slash at it with the razor. You remind yourself that bleeding to death is exactly like going to sleep. Or so you've heard. And that is all you want. Sleep. Nothing more than sleep.

When you open your eyes, you are surprised at how much blood you see. The sink is so covered with it that at first you think you've dropped a red towel over its edge. For a moment, the realization of what you've done sweeps over you, but then you think of sleep, of being free of the whispers, and you smile. You watch the blood pump through the lips you've slashed in your arm and you wait for the first sign of weakness to overtake you. Anticipation fills you as the blood pulses out of the wound, but you feel no weaker. You back away from the sink, your other hand still clutching the razor, and sit down on the toilet. The blood falls like a dropped roll of Christmas ribbon, uncoiling from your arm. You feel no closer to sleep than yesterday. Now the blood slows. Not gushing anymore, it only drips and then thins into a rivulet until finally the wound is nothing but an empty mouth.

A man standing in the doorway grins at you, but when you look up, you see only shadows. The darkness beyond bulges and falls. The voice whispers in your ear and you feel hot dry breath on the back of your neck. You throw the razor down and leap up.

In the closet, you tear out your wife's underwear drawer and dig until you find the pistol you bought for her. She always hated it; never carried it. Now you're glad. You drop it once, the blood on your hands still slippery. You pick it up and load it and quickly put it in your mouth and pull the trigger. The pain of the hot metal ripping through the back of your neck is terrible. You feel as if you've been hit on the head with a hammer. But still you cannot sleep. You pull the trigger again, the fire from the muzzle singeing your tongue, filling your nose with the awful stench of living, burning flesh. But still you cannot sleep.

You throw the gun down and run to the front door. At the stairwell, you run up. On the roof, you hurry to the edge and without thinking throw yourself to the street six stories below. You hit the concrete with a terrible wet crack. Splinters of pain shoot through your legs and arms, but already you are standing. You hobble up the sidewalk, knowing only you want to get away from the whispering. You must sleep. You don't even notice the people calling out to you, the people staring and pointing.

Three blocks away, you hear the distant hoot of a train whistle. Pain flaring in your crushed leg, you hobble forward as quickly as you can manage. You are still a block away when the whistle sounds again and the bells of the crossing arm ring. Traffic stops before the pulsing red lights, but not you. Your feet twist in the gravel as you pour on one last burst of speed and throw yourself onto the rails as the juggernaut roars through the dark and its front wheels slice across your legs and chest. You hear bones snap and flesh tear and suddenly the train screeches to a halt, sparks flying in the dark. You tumble from the tracks and spin around. In the dark under the train you see the rest of your body as it is crushed and swept away like newspaper in rain. You look down and see your right arm is only a stump now. Below your throat, the white bones of your ribcage poke out from meat so dark and red it looks black. Your left arm, though, remains intact, and even now you grab the hard ground and pull yourself forward. A block ahead, you see traffic whipping past. If only you can reach it.

You pull and pull, your flesh scraping through the gravel, now onto the sidewalk. What blood you have in you is left behind like a snail trail. You hear people screaming; somewhere in the distance, sirens. At the corner, a man looks down at you and then falls to the ground, clutching his chest. His eyes flutter closed and you envy him his sleep. At the curb, you pull yourself over the edge. You look up and see a truck coming. Quickly, you pull yourself onto the asphalt and put your ear to it. The truck bears down on you and its headlights blind you and you close your eyes as the tires plow across your skull, crushing it flat. The darkness engulfs you. But still you are not asleep. And now you realize you will never sleep. And in the darkness, you hear the whispers. And you feel their hands touching you. And you know you are theirs.

A Tither
of Mint

THERE ONCE WAS A YOUNG WOMAN WHO GAVE BIRTH TO a cyclops: a boy with only one eye in the center of his face, just above his nose, as clear and blue as the heart of a glacier. Because the one-eyed boy's parents were good Christians, they each saw the child as a sign from God: the mother was sure the boy had been born deformed because of some sin the father had committed; the father was sure they had been given the boy to test the strength of their love. And so the mother hated the one-eyed boy because of his deformity and the father loved him because of it.

Because the town was a good Christian town, the mother insisted no one know about the child. She was sure the neighbors would talk behind her back, trying to figure out what secret sin had created such a monster, and she had spent too long with an unspoiled reputation to have it ruined by something that certainly was not her fault. The mother wanted to get rid of the child, to set it afloat on the river outside of town the way Moses's mother had done with him, but the father wouldn't allow it. He was afraid giving up the child would bring a rain of fire and brimstone on their house. Besides, he told his wife, that would be murder, and at least they both agreed on the Ten Commandments. So they kept the child, but as a secret. They

paid the town doctor a small sum of money to back up their story
the child had died at birth, then buried an empty coffin in the town
churchyard.

When they returned home, the father told his wife that if anything
ever happened to the boy, he would turn her out. Because she had
come from a poor family and her husband was set to inherit a large
fortune once his father passed on, she promised to take care of the
child. She did this in only the most rudimentary way, however, often
beating the child with a sock filled with sand so there would be no
bruises.

As the boy grew, the mother and father tried to have more children,
but couldn't. The mother blamed her barrenness on the one-eyed boy,
saying it had poisoned her womb with its deformity. But the father,
who sometimes believed even his wife had been sent to him by God
to test his love, didn't ask her to stop talking that way, only to lower
her voice.

In the night, the father, kept awake by black clouds of guilt, sneaked
into the boy's room and read to him secretly and explained to him he
couldn't go outside because he was special. This might have made the
boy feel better, but the boy's mother had already told him he wasn't
special, he was a freak of nature, abnormal, hideous to everyone, a
thing to be spat upon and trampled down if he ever went outside
with other people. And so the boy grew, never permitted to leave the
house, always locked in his attic room, staring out the window at the
town below, wishing God had given him two eyes instead of one so
he could be free.

After many years, the mother grew old and tired of waiting for her
father-in-law to die. She wanted the money now, so they could leave
town and move to the city. This, of course, was a secret. Her husband
believed she loved him for him, not for his money.

Then, one day shortly after the boy's twelfth birthday, a traveling
carnival came through town, and the mother, coming back from the

grocery store, was drawn to it by the smell of popcorn and cotton candy and the sound of the calliope and the snap of the canvas tents. The carnival reminded her of a time from her youth, when her father had actually saved enough money for her family to go to the state fair. It had been the best day of her life, and as she approached the carnival she felt better than she had in years. She paid the nickel admission and went inside, wandering around, wide-eyed. At the freak tent, she stopped short and stared at the canvas banners—The Spark Eater! Skeletoid! The Human Ape!—and she realized here was the answer to her prayers. No normal family would have taken her one-eyed boy for adoption, but this? This was the boy's real family. It always had been.

Hating herself for having wasted twelve years of her life taking care of that monster, she looked about frantically for an employee. When she spotted a dwarf at the "Test Your Strength" booth, she hurried over and asked where she could find the owner of the carnival. Using his directions, she finally located the man, who called himself Doktor Pernicious. She explained her situation, and the good Doktor agreed to pay her $1,000 for the boy if he was everything she said he was. He was, she reassured him, and she promised to return.

That night, the mother secretly had a drink of whiskey, then went to her bedroom stripped naked. She and her husband hadn't made love in so long he was on his knees without being asked. She got him drunk and, after forcing herself to have sex with him, waited until he passed out, then sneaked upstairs and took the one-eyed boy and his things across town to the carnival. Doktor Pernicious was most pleased and duly paid the $1,000 he had promised.

The next morning, the mother woke the father up screaming their boy was gone—they had forgotten to lock his door and he had run away. She showed him a note she had forged, and even though the father suspected what had happened, he was so tired of having his love tested that he said he believed her.

When they went to church later, the woman saw the carnival had gone, and she sat in the pew with the $1,000 in her purse and sang hymns with a vigor she had never displayed before.

She

In the darkness
She comes to me
From the forest
Across the lea
To rap on my window
Ever, oh, so gently

Not a sound on her lips
Save a moan of dark pleasure
That does mine increase
Measure by measure

Her pale skin
Like blue moonbeams
Her crimson lips
Like freshly cut flesh seams
Her hollow eyes
Of blackest coal
Her willowy hair
A body without soul

On my hot skin
She brings her cold fingers
Her ice cools my fire
The longer she lingers

Faster and faster
Until burst white suns in my head
Then quietly she rises
From the still-trembling bed

Out again she goes
Until the sun sets tomorrow
As my pleasure melts
And freezes into sorrow

To sleep I wander
To dream of her again
Not caring whence she comes
Not caring where she has been

For I know I'll hear her rapping
Every night until I die
And then with her always
Forever will I lie

Mine
Now

BLAKE THOUGHT HE AND THE OLD MAN WERE WAITING FOR the same thing. But when the bus arrived, the old man stood up and hurried away, as if realizing he had forgotten something. Blake saw that indeed he had. The shoebox-sized parcel, wrapped in brown paper and twine, was still on the bench where it had been between them.

"Excuse me," Blake called after the old man. He lifted the parcel, surprised at how heavy it was, and held it up. "You forgot this."

The old man looked over his shoulder and shook his head. "Not mine," he said. "I thought it was yours. I guess it is now."

Before Blake could say anything else, the old man turned around and rushed off.

Blake stood still for a moment, as if posing for a photograph, then moved toward the bus reflexively. When he realized he still held the package, he moved to set it back on the bench, then reconsidered with a shrug and boarded. *The old man is right,* he thought. *Whatever it is, it's mine now.*

He tucked the parcel under his arm, showed his pass to the driver, then found an empty seat halfway down on the right-hand side, next to a lady in a dark blue sweater.

He smiled at her as he sat down and held the parcel in his lap. She did not return his smile.

"That's stealing, you know," she said to him.

He frowned and looked at her. "Excuse me?"

"What you did. That's stealing. You stole that package."

"But that old man said it wasn't his."

"It's not yours, is it?"

"Well, no."

"See? Stealing."

Blake suddenly felt guilty. Then he remembered: he had arrived at the bus stop first. The old man had come after him. The package had not been there until the old man. So it must have been his. He quickly explained all this to the lady, then added, "And since he told me it was mine now, it can't really be stealing, isn't that right?"

She looked at him like his first-grade teacher and sighed. "But I heard him tell you it wasn't his," she said. "So he had no more right to give it to you than you had to take it." She looked away then, as if she were the one who was ashamed.

Blake confronted the parcel in his lap, sorry now that he hadn't left it.

"What should I do, then?" he asked.

"Take it back. Whoever left it there will probably come back to look for it."

Blake checked his watch. If he got off the bus now, he would only lose fifteen minutes at the most. As usual, he had half an hour to spare. He reached over the lady and pulled the cable to ring the bell and light up the "Stop Requested" panel. As he sat back down, the lady smiled at him.

"You're doing the right thing," she said.

Blake nodded unenthusiastically. Part of him felt like he should thank her, but for what, he didn't know. Maybe for not making a citizen's arrest right there. She seemed the type. Instead, he mumbled

"See you later" as he stood and moved to the rear exit. The bus hissed to a halt and he pushed the doors open and stepped down.

He checked his watch again. The next bus would arrive at his stop at 7:29 a.m. It was now 7:17. That was barely twelve minutes to walk two miles. He would have to walk ten miles an hour to make that. He knew he wouldn't be able to. He would have to wait for the 7:44 now. *Unless I can catch the uptown bus,* he thought, and hurried to the corner to cross the street.

While he waited for the light, he tucked the parcel under his right arm and realized that in the space of only a few minutes, his entire routine had been disrupted. He had been called a thief. Now he was trying to do the right thing by putting the package back where he had found it and he would be late for work and for that he would get in trouble. Mr. Travers wouldn't care about his noble deed, and Blake would have another undeserved black mark scratched onto his permanent record.

The more he thought about it, the angrier he got. He soon convinced himself the lady on the bus had been wrong. What he had done was not stealing. Finders keepers, losers weepers, right? He had found that package fair and square and the old man had been right— it was his now.

He heard the uptown bus, but by the time he snapped out of his trance and actually saw it, he had missed the light, and the bus roared away, leaving behind only a black cloud of diesel smoke.

Blake gritted his teeth and turned in the opposite direction. Now he would have to walk back to his stop. He pushed the parcel under his left arm and crossed the street quickly.

He grew more frustrated with each step. He decided that he should just open the package after all. Maybe there was something valuable inside. As if in answer to this thought, he saw a pawn shop on the next block. Smiling, he stopped and sat down on the steps of a fourplex.

He set the package across his knees and stared at it, rubbing his hands together, anxious to tear through the wrinkled brown paper and find out what was inside. But just as his fingers pulled off the twine, he heard the lady on the bus again: "That's stealing, you know." Only this time, it was his mother's voice. His shoulders drooped. *Suppose I open it and just take a look. Then I could wrap it back up and return it to the bus bench.* This seemed reasonable. If it was worthless, he could put it back knowing that his curiosity had been satisfied. And if it was valuable, well, then . . .

In spite of all this justification, he still knew deep in the pit of his stomach that it was wrong, but he ripped the paper off anyway, all in one stroke, so there would be no chance for second thoughts.

He smiled when he saw it was a shoebox. People put money in shoeboxes, didn't they? He swallowed dryly and lifted the top off. He blinked in disbelief. It wasn't money. It was better. The object inside was solid gold. It had to be. It was a statue, about eleven inches tall, of a figure with four faces and four arms. His first thought was that it was South American, but the longer he looked at it, the less sure he became. Asian, maybe. African, perhaps. "Who the hell cares?" he said out loud, turning it over again. When he realized he was holding several pounds of gold up for everyone to see, he shoved it back in the box and slapped the lid on.

He couldn't imagine the pawn shop would give him what it was really worth, but surely they could at least tell him if it was real gold.

Fear knotted his gut. Blake was afraid they would tell him it wasn't. They would say it was lead that had been spray-painted. He told himself it was simply too good to be true, but the words echoed hollowly in his head, weightless. He didn't believe them because he couldn't. The four-faced thing was gold. It was worth a lot of money. Money he would soon have. Then he could quit his job. Go on a trip. He was at the next intersection before he realized he had gotten up and started walking.

Before he reached the pawn shop, however, he saw the old man coming straight toward him. Blake froze. For a moment, he couldn't believe his eyes. He blinked, thinking his imagination was playing tricks on him. But it wasn't. The old man was still there—still coming straight toward him. Blake ducked into the pawn shop as fast as he could, but it was too late, the old man had seen him. A moment later, the door opened and he came in.

"I'm glad I found you," the old man said, out of breath.

I knew it, Blake thought. *It all was too good to be true. He's going to tell me the package really is his after all and he wants it back. I should have known. I've got bad luck for a shadow.* "Really?" he said. "Why?"

The old man's eyes flashed toward the shoebox. "You opened it, eh."

Blake nodded, then looked over his shoulder. The clerks behind the counter were staring at them. Afraid of a scene, Blake went past the old man, back outside to the sidewalk. The old man followed him quickly.

"I suppose you're going to tell me this is yours now."

"No," the old man said.

Blake stared at him. "What?"

"Let me say first that I'm terribly sorry to have gotten you all mixed up in this, but I didn't have a choice."

"What are you talking about?"

"You saw what was inside the box?"

"I thought you said it wasn't yours."

"I lied."

"So it is yours?"

"Not exactly. Not anymore, thank God. You stole it from me."

"It was not stealing," Blake shouted.

"Say that if you want but it was. I'm glad, frankly. I owe you my life because of it."

The old man wasn't making any sense. Blake looked around, searching for a hidden camera crew. "Am I on TV or something?"

The old man laughed bitterly. "No. I wish you were. You didn't recognize the statue?"

"No. Should I have?"

"It was in the papers. It was stolen from Walker Museum two weeks ago."

"What?"

The old man nodded. "By an associate of mine. A man named Trent. A professional thief. Like me. We all tried to warn him. But he wouldn't listen." The old man's eyes went to the shoebox. "That thing is cursed."

Blake looked for the TV cameras again. "Cursed?"

The old man nodded. "Trent is dead because of it. The curse falls on whoever steals the statue. The only way to save yourself is if someone else steals it from you."

"How did you get it, then?"

"I stole it."

"Even though you knew it was cursed."

"Because of that. After Trent died, my brother stole the statue from him. He thought it was safe. But it wasn't. And since he stole it, he would have died. So I stole it from him, see. To save his life. Then I got you to steal it from me."

Even though he didn't believe him, Blake played along. "So why didn't you give it to someone?"

"It doesn't work that way. Don't you get it?"

"I get it all right. You're not going to come right out and ask for it back. You're going to try to scare me into giving it back."

The old man backed up a step. "No," he said, holding up his hands as if warding off a blow.

A wave of nausea broke loose in Blake's gut and rolled down both legs, turning them to ice. The old man's reaction had been too sudden and honest not to be true. He was genuinely afraid of the statue. Blake told himself this had to be some kind of prank or hoax or something. But then the 7:29 bus roared past, a symbol of concrete reality that he couldn't explain away or disbelieve, and another wave of nausea washed over him.

"How long?" Blake asked.

"Twenty-four hours."

"What?"

"I'm sorry," the old man said. "After you got on the bus, I realized what I had done and it made me sick. I traded my brother's life for yours because I couldn't give up my own."

Anger exploded between his ears and Blake stepped toward the old man, pushing the box against his chest. "You have to take it back, then."

"I can't. I told you. It wouldn't do you any good. Somebody has to steal it from you."

"So steal it from me. I'll set it down. You grab it and run."

"That would be like giving it to me. It's not the same."

"But that's what you did."

"Not exactly. I told you it wasn't mine and you still took it."

"Because you told me to."

"You always do what strangers tell you?"

Blake looked away, ashamed. He knew the old man was right. The same way he had known the lady on the bus was right. Why else had he gotten off? Everything beyond that was pretend.

"So what am I supposed to do?"

"Get somebody else to steal it from you. But know that whoever does will die because of it. I'm sorry."

The old man ran off again, leaving Blake alone, exactly as he had at the bus stop. When Blake looked through the windows of the pawn shop, he saw the clerks inside, still staring at him. He stared back at them until they looked away, then dropped his shoulders and shuffled along the sidewalk back toward his own stop, even though he didn't really need to go there any longer. Why should he? If he only had twenty-four hours to live, did he really want to spend them at work? Of course not. What he really wanted was to find that lady from the bus and get her to steal the statue from him. Even as he imagined the scenario, he knew it could never come true. She would never steal anything. She was probably the kind of lady who, if given too much change at the store, tells the cashier and gives the free money back.

But not Jack Travers.

Blake stopped walking. No. Not Jack Travers. In fact, just the other day, Travers had been bragging about exactly such an incident. The clerk at the sandwich shop had mistaken his $10 bill for a $20 bill and had given him $13 in change. "I got paid for eating lunch today," he had bragged for the rest of the afternoon. Blake remembered thinking Travers had all the luck. Now he was thinking that might change very soon.

Three blocks ahead, Blake spotted a covered bus shelter, and he hurried to it. The 7:44 arrived five minutes late, but Blake didn't care. In fact, for the first time in his life, Blake wished it had been later. He really wanted Travers to be mad at him for being late to work. He was sure that would inspire Travers to seek a special kind of revenge, such as stealing something from him.

Blake got off the bus at 8:15 and took his time walking the rest of the way to work. He had never been this late before. To make sure everything would go according to the scenario he had come up with during his bus ride, he checked the parking lot to confirm Travers was there (he was), then made a show of sneaking through the side door.

He was halfway down the hall when Travers came out of his office. "Mister Corning," Travers said in that particularly proud tone of his. It was the same tone he had used when bragging about getting paid to eat lunch. "Do you realize that you are more than half an hour late?"

Blake stopped and turned around, acting like he was trying to hide the shoebox. "I know, sir. I'm terribly sorry. I fully expect to have my pay docked for the prorated amount."

"That's right," Travers said. "Because otherwise you are stealing from the company, isn't that right?"

Blake nodded. "Right. Because if I'm getting paid and I'm not here doing my work, that's the same as taking money from the register."

"Exactly," Travers said, then he raised his voice a notch. "Like those employees who play computer games on company time. Thieves, the lot of you." Travers looked back at Blake. For a moment, he worried that his boss wasn't going to ask about the shoebox, then he saw his eyes flash to it. "What's that?"

"Oh, this?" Blake asked. "Just something I found." Quickly, Blake turned around and hurried to his office, hoping he could make Travers curious enough to perform one of his "surprise" inspections while Blake was in the bathroom or at lunch.

To fuel the fire, Blake sat down behind his desk and immediately began e-mailing his co-workers about his remarkable morning. He told everyone how he had found the shoebox with the gold statue inside. They all wanted to see it, but they knew they didn't dare come by Blake's office. Not unless they were on break. Otherwise, they would be stealing.

At 11:45, Blake tucked the shoebox under his desk, then pulled it back out far enough so that it could be easily seen. He put on his hat and coat, carefully locked his office door (Travers had his own key), and left for lunch.

He couldn't eat. Not because he was afraid of the curse, but because he was so excited that his plan might actually work and he would be rid of Travers once and for all. He supposed he should have left his office door open because that would have increased his chances of having the statue stolen, but he really only wanted Travers to be the one.

He pushed his half-eaten hamburger into the trash, took one last

sip of soda, then hurried back to the office. He arrived fifteen minutes early.

Everyone else, except the receptionist, was at lunch. Blake held his
breath as he went down the hall to his office. He let out a sigh and
smiled when he saw his door was open. His smile grew when he saw
the shoebox was missing. It had worked! It had really worked!

Blake used his hands to push the smile from his face and furrowed
his brow in anger. "Who stole it?!" he said. "Who stole it?!" he called
again, louder, trying to imitate outrage as best he could. "Mister
Travers!" he shouted and rushed back into the hallway.

Travers was already there, along with two police officers. Blake's
first thought was that they had caught Travers stealing the statue
from his office and had arrested him. But he could see they were with
Travers, not hauling him away.

"I read your e-mails this morning," Travers said.

"So you know about what I found?"

"I didn't, exactly. Not until I took a look at it myself. Then I knew.
It's the statue that was stolen from the Walker Museum."

Blake gulped. Another wave of nausea froze his limbs.

Travers went on. "Now, I assured the police here that you are not
capable of performing a burglary like that yourself. Nor do I believe
you are involved in any way other than what you described. But the
simple fact is that I cannot tolerate people like you on my staff."

Blake was too busy trying to put it all together to fully compre-
hend what Travers was saying. "People like me?"

"Thieves. People who take things that don't belong to them. People
who find things and don't turn them in to the proper authorities.
Which is what I have done, since you didn't. And now these gen-
tlemen will make sure that the artifact is returned to the museum."

"What?"

"That's right. You should be glad. Would you rather I told them I
thought you had stolen it?"

"No."

"I didn't think so. Now they'd like to ask you a few questions. And after you're finished with them, I'd like you to clean out your office and pick up your final check from me."

"Final check?"

Travers nodded. "As of right now, you are no longer an employee of this company."

Blake smiled again. Only this time, his smile got bigger and bigger until it turned into a laugh.

Travers looked at the two police officers, then back at Blake. "Why on earth are you laughing?"

"Because," Blake choked. "I wished I would never see you again. And I got my wish. That's why. I got exactly what I wished for."

Elegiac

REBECCA **K**ADISH STOOD BEHIND THE LONG GLASS COUNTER inside Kadish's Kosher Deli #1. She watched the door, her head set on her soft, wide shoulders like a stone on a mound of clay, her eyes tired and gray—eyes that had seen too much and had no pity left in them; they had filmed over, like pools of standing water. She absently twisted her wedding ring on her finger, its edges as smooth and comfortable as her marriage had become after forty-seven years. Her daughter, Stacy, came in from the back room with a fat jar of pickles and set it on the shiny steel countertop. She shook her short brown hair to one side and looked at her mother pitifully. Her eyes were too young to have seen too much; they were still capable of pity. "For God's sake, Ma," she said, setting a handwritten "$1/ea." sign on the jar. "He'll be here."

"I'm worried," Rebecca said. "Look at that weather." Outside, rain lashed the windows, jerked by the gusting wind into bullwhips made of water.

"The other store is only four blocks away," Stacy said. "What can happen between here and there?"

"Ninety percent of all accidents happen within one mile of home," Rebecca said. "I heard that on the TV the other night."

"We aren't at home."

Rebecca wanted to snap back "This place practically is home," but before she could respond, the front door opened and a great circle of black pushed through. It was her husband, Horace. Rebecca straightened herself as if preparing for battle, rubbing her hard white hands on the front of her mustard-stained apron. Her worry, now denied its foundation, collapsed into anger. "Where have you been?" she demanded. "The other store is only four blocks away. And don't you dare shake that umbrella in here."

Horace looked at her from the doorway, his beige topcoat dark with water. "Whatever you say, dear," he said, and he carefully folded the umbrella, hanging it on the hook by the door along with his hat and coat. He scratched his bald head and smiled as he approached the counter, his blue eyes huge and alive behind his thick glasses. They looked like busy insects under a magnifying glass.

"And what is it with that smile lately?" Rebecca turned to Stacy. "Everything now, he smiles at. Like a crazy man. That's just what I need: for my husband to lose his head. With two years left at the most."

"Ma!" Stacy said. "Don't talk like that. You two are young still."

"No we're not. That's why I say you better start having babies so we can meet our grandkids before you put us in the earth, God bless us." Rebecca faced Horace again. "So? Does it take so long to walk four blocks?"

"I've been at the travel agent," Horace said, smiling.

"Travel agent? What for?"

"These," he said, reaching into his plaid sport coat and pulling out a long white envelope. "We're going on a trip."

"A trip! We just got back from a cruise a month ago."

"You always say we don't travel enough."

"There is such a thing as traveling too much, you know."

"Nonsense," Stacy said, enviously grabbing the envelope from her father's soft, thick hand. She peeled it open as if its contents were for her and peered inside. Her face, bright with anticipation, dimmed into a frown. Slowly, she looked up. "Germany?" she whispered, dumbfounded, as if it were a four-letter word. "You swore you'd never go back there."

Horace shrugged and smiled. But his wife's face hardened and bunched like a withered apple. She snatched the tickets from her daughter and stared at them. "What's going on?" she said deliberately, her watery eyes rippling as if something dark had passed under their surface. "What's got into you? Everything's crazy lately. First it's 'sell the other store,' now it's off to Germany."

"Sell the other store?" Stacy asked. "What?"

Horace shrugged and smiled. "It's sold."

"When did this happen?"

"Last week."

"But you didn't have it open two months."

"Now my daughter's going to read me my rights? What's it come to when a man can't do what he wants and not hear all about it from everyone?" Even this he said with a smile.

"But why?" Stacy asked.

"What do I need a reason for? Age is enough. I'm going to be sixty-five, I don't need another deli. This one's plenty."

"Okay, okay," Stacy said, throwing her hands up. "I've had it. I hope John and I aren't like you two after forty-seven years." She went into the back room again, her shoulders already starting to sag like her mother's.

Rebecca looked at her husband, her gray eyes searching his smiling face. "You going to tell me now what you want to go to Germany for?" she said flatly.

"Don't you want to? It's our home—where we were born."

"Also almost where we died, God bless us."

"Don't you remember how you used to talk about going back?

When we were first married, in the night, you would hold me and cry and say you wanted to go see your friends."

"And you refused. Said you'd die before you'd set foot on Nazi dirt again."

"So I changed my mind. This is what I get for giving you a present?"

"What are you talking about?"

"I thought this would be a surprise. I've been planning it now for how long?"

"So that's what with all this smiling," Rebecca said.

Horace shrugged and smiled and stared at his wife across the shiny steel top of the long glass counter. She turned up the corners of her loose mouth in a look of constipated disgust, still nagged by the feeling that he was hiding something. And she didn't like it. Not one bit.

Two days later, Rebecca followed her husband to the bank for traveler's checks. They had left Stacy in charge of the deli. Horace drove the Cadillac; Rebecca drove the Chevy. She thought it was strange he wanted to take both cars, but he'd told her he had another surprise for her. When she'd asked what it was, he'd smiled and shrugged and said, "Then it wouldn't be a surprise." All the way to the bank she worried, her eyes darkening, sinking into her hard face like black pebbles falling down a well.

Suddenly, he turned the wrong way down a street. She honked at him, but he kept driving. He had told her to follow him no matter what he did, and she was forced to cut off another car to make the turn. Horns blared and she sat up straight and leaned over the wheel, angry, wondering what on earth her husband was doing. Going crazy, she reminded herself, almost kidding. *He's going crazy,* she thought again, not kidding at all this time. He turned down another street, then another, until Rebecca had no idea where they were. They passed an unfamiliar shopping mall and rows of tract houses that all looked the same and Rebecca returned to worrying, seriously wondering if her husband really had gone nuts. She was thinking of all the crazy things he might do when he turned again, into a car lot this time, a "TOYOTA" sign looming overhead like some giant sentinel. "What is this?" she said under her breath, but she followed him in anyway.

He parked the Cadillac in front of a door labeled "Office" and went inside before she could pull up next to him and park. As she hoisted herself from the Chevy, Horace emerged from the office beside a young black man in a white shirt and red tie. The salesman smiled as he approached, his teeth as white as his shirt. "Hello, Mrs. Kadish," he said, holding out his hand. "It's a pleasure to finally meet you. I've heard so much about you."

She was almost too angry now to be polite, but she took his hand anyway, then frowned and let it go. "What's going on?" she demanded, turning her big face on Horace like a wild animal rearing back, ready to strike. But he only smiled and shrugged. Over his shoulder, Rebecca saw two men in blue jumpsuits come out of the office. One got into the Chevy, the other got into the Cadillac. "Hey," she shouted. "What are they doing with our cars?"

"Not yours anymore," the black man said, cocking his head and winking. "This one is." He motioned like a game show host behind him, and Rebecca turned as another man in a blue jumpsuit pulled up in a white Toyota and hopped out.

Rebecca faced Horace. "Have you gone out of your head?"

"I traded our cars in," Horace said, shrugging dismissively and smiling. "You said you wanted one of these."

"When did I say that?"

"More than once," Horace said, still smiling. "The other day was the last time. You saw one in the parking lot at the grocery store. You said it would be nice to have one."

"But what do we do now, without two cars?"

"What do we need two cars for?" Horace said. "Double the trouble, all it is. Twice the insurance. Twice the gas."

Rebecca didn't know what to think as the man in the blue jump-suit approached her and held out the keys. "But all our things in the other cars."

"I cleaned them out last night," Horace said. "Stop worrying so much."

Horace and the black salesman exchanged glances and smiled. They seemed amused by Rebecca's behavior. This only made her angrier. She snatched the keys from the man in the blue jumpsuit, then said, "I hope this is it with all your surprises." She started toward the car. "We'll never get to the bank on time now."

"Oh, don't worry," Horace said. "I went yesterday. I only told you we were going to the bank today so you wouldn't ask where we were going." He smiled at her and got into their new car. Reluctantly, still angry, she climbed in with him.

The next day, Horace left the deli early with a friend, and when Rebecca got home, she saw a white van parked in the driveway. A man in white overalls stood at their front door. Another stood on a ladder outside the living-room window. The door and windows were open.

"What in heaven's name?" she shouted, driving onto the lawn in a panic. She didn't even take the keys out of the ignition before she threw the door open and headed for the house. "Hey, you!" she shouted as she lumbered toward the men. "Who are you? What are you doing to my house?" The men looked at her as if at some crazy woman, then at each other. And then, as if she weren't there, they went back to work. Rebecca couldn't believe this was happening. She turned and shouted at the street, "Call the police! I'm being robbed!"

"Rebecca," Horace called behind her.

She turned toward him, shaking, afraid. She wanted him to hold her, but when she saw he was smiling, she got angry again. "You," she said, pointing one hard white finger at him. "What have you done now?"

"Calm down," Horace said. "I asked them to come here. They're putting in an alarm system."

"Alarm system!" she repeated.

"For when we're gone."

"Stacy will be here. She always stays at our house when we go away."

Horace shook his head. "Not this time. She and John have their own lives to lead. Now come inside before the neighbors really do call the police." He approached her slowly and put one arm around her shoulders.

Rebecca shook it off angrily, as if it were an annoying insect, then looked over her shoulder and saw Mrs. Winston peering through the window from her house across the street. When Mrs. Winston saw Rebecca looking at her, she dropped the curtains back across the glass. Rebecca turned around, her forehead bunched into a worried frown. The men in white jumpsuits looked at her as she passed by, but she only shook her head.

The day they were to leave for Germany, Rebecca awakened and found her husband's bed neatly made. Her heart kicked once inside the deep flesh of her chest and she quickly threw back the covers. He never got up before she did. She looked at the digital clock on the nightstand between their beds and saw it was a few minutes after five. Panicked, she lifted herself to the floor and crossed the dim bedroom to the closet for her robe. The sliding door stood open in front of Horace's half. It was empty. Everything was gone: the shirts, the pants, the suitcoats, the ties, the shoes. Her eyes widened and her head sank into her clay-soft shoulders. *He's left me,* she thought. *Gone off with some other woman. This trip was supposed to distract me. To hide his guilt.* She heard something thump in the kitchen. He was still there. She would catch him.

Rebecca lumbered down the hall, her steps pounding the floor like drums before battle. She entered the kitchen, expecting to see

Horace sneaking through the dark laden with suitcases, but all the lights were on and the smell of fresh coffee touched her nose. Horace turned from the ironing board, still dressed in his pajamas. He smiled at her. "Good morning, dear," he said. "Coffee's ready." With a polite shrug, he turned and continued ironing.

Rebecca took another step forward, her eyes suddenly wide, flitting about the brightly lit kitchen like flies, lighting here on a pile of shirts, there on a line of pants. The table was covered with newspaper and his shoes were in two neat rows like soldiers on parade. A rag spotted with black sat bunched near them. She realized that he had polished them all. Slowly, she walked around the ironing board. When Horace looked up at her, he smiled. She reached her hand out and felt his forehead.

"What are you doing?" he asked, his smile widening.

"Checking for the fever," Rebecca said. "What is this?"

"I'm ironing."

"I can see that. What for?"

"I want everything to be neat."

"And you talk about how much I take on a trip!"

Horace laughed. "I'm not taking all these things."

"Then what are you doing?"

He shrugged. "I thought I might as well do it all while I was at it. No sense leaving a job half done."

Rebecca couldn't help a laugh: a short, sharp, pitiless bark of a laugh. "This is my Horace? We have half a deck in the backyard you didn't finish last summer. The garage roof still leaks. The meat slicer in the deli is good only for a paperweight. The—"

"All done," Horace said quietly.

"What?"

"All done. The people who did Mrs. Winston's deck are coming while we're gone. Stacy took the meat slicer to the shop, and I fixed the garage roof the other day."

Rebecca's shoulders sagged in disbelief.

"Now have some coffee and finish packing," Horace said. "Stacy is coming to take us to the airport at ten."

"Horace, please," Rebecca said, almost begging. "Tell me what is going on."

"Nothing, dear," he said.

Afraid to do anything else, Rebecca did as she was told.

After they arrived in Berlin, they checked into a hotel and stayed one night to get over the jet lag. The next day, they ate breakfast in silence, Rebecca too worried to say anything. Horace had done nothing but smile since their arrival. After breakfast, they caught a cab back to the airport. Horace said they were going to start in Munich and were catching a commuter flight. This made Rebecca even more afraid. Outside Munich was Dachau: where he had been. Where they both had lost their parents and their brothers and sisters and aunts and uncles. They had both been young during the war, not seventeen, strong enough to stand the forced labor, God bless them. They had met after the liberation, on one of the Allied trains to France. They had needed each other then. And Rebecca liked to think that they still did, but after these last two weeks, she didn't know what was happening to them.

They flew to Munich in silence and got a rental car at the airport, then drove to their hotel.

The next morning, Rebecca couldn't eat. Horace didn't seem to notice and instead smiled at her and reminisced about the days before the war. He talked incessantly about how no one had known what was coming, and after breakfast, as he led the way to their rental car, she asked where they were going now.

"Dachau," he said, smiling brightly.

Rebecca stopped short, completely afraid. She wanted to do something—needed to—but she didn't know what. "And if I say no?" she said, her strong voice shaking.

Horace stopped and faced her. Germans hurried past them in both directions, on their way about their business. "Then I will. You can wait for me at the hotel." He turned and started along the sidewalk again.

"Why?" Rebecca called after him.

He stopped again but did not face her. She stared at his wide back, at his fat, sloping shoulders. He shrugged. "Because I need to. That's all. Because I need to." He faced her again. For the first time, he wasn't smiling. His pale bald head shone in the crisp sunlight like white fire. He looked as if he had a halo. "So?" he said.

Too worried to let him go alone, too afraid to go with him, Rebecca went anyway.

They arrived at Dachau and parked in the big parking lot and went to the visitor's center and wandered through. Horace stared at the black-and-white photos on the wall like a detective searching for hidden clues. Rebecca couldn't bear to remember, and so she concentrated on her husband's face. She grew more worried and afraid by the moment, following him wherever he went, clutching his hand tightly. What frightened her most of all was that she thought he looked happy.

With a smile, he signed them up for the next tour, and they waited in silence on a bench outside. When a shrill voice announced their start time, they stood up together and joined their group.

After, the guide thanked them for coming, and they wandered back toward the parking lot, not holding hands anymore. At the border of the camp, a security guard stood watch. In his black uniform, he reminded Rebecca of the SS guards she had tried so hard to forget, and suddenly she hated her husband for everything: for selling the other deli, for trading in their cars, for bringing her here, for making her go through this. She liked their life the way it had been. Why did he want to change everything? Her anger grew inside her like water running down a narrowing pipe, the pressure building. She knew he had a real reason and he simply wasn't telling her. She resolved not to take another step until he explained himself and, for the second time that day, she stopped short. She stared at the ground and shook her head and stamped her foot on the hard, dark earth.

When she looked up, she saw that he had gone on ahead toward the gate. He stopped near the black-clad guard and looked up at him. The guard looked down, his blond hair gold in the sun, his blue eyes too deep set to be anything but suspicious. And then, without warning, Horace spread his arms and put them around the guard and stood on the toes of his carefully polished shoes and kissed him. The guard was too stunned to do anything. He stood there stiffly as Horace pulled his fat arms from around him and smiled and nodded and continued on toward the car. Rebecca looked around to make sure no one knew the man who had kissed the guard was with her, then hurried through the gate.

When she got to the car, she saw Horace already inside, in the passenger seat, his hat in his lap, his hands folded neatly over it, his eyes closed. Shaking her head angrily—she had no intention of driving in this crazy foreign country—she pounded on the window. But Horace just sat there, smiling again as if satisfied with himself, eyes still closed. She tried to open the door, but it was locked. Hurrying around to the driver's side, she yanked the door open and threw herself in. "What is the meaning of this? I have had it with you! I can't take it anymore."

Horace faced her, still smiling, eyes still closed, then bowed his head slowly.

"Answer me!" she shouted.

But Horace remained silent, and when Rebecca leaned toward him, he tipped over and slumped against her heavily.

But for the Grace of God

"**D**ID YOU EVER THINK BUT FOR THE GRACE OF **G**OD YOU'D be a serial killer?"

As if on cue, the street lamp outside the window behind Tony went out. Sean hoped it wasn't the grace of God leaving.

"What?" he said.

"You know," Tony said. "That if you weren't . . . I don't know . . . all together, that you'd be a serial killer. I don't mean one of those sickos like Dahmer, eating your victims and all that."

"Of course not," Sean said. "You'd be one of those normal sickos who just kills people." He forced a laugh and hoped Tony would go along with him. He didn't.

"Exactly. People who deserve it. Like that Green River guy in Seattle."

Sean pushed a bead of sweat away from his eye. "Green River guy?"

"Killed hookers. He understood trash like that doesn't deserve to live. Lot of people like them around, know what I mean? People who don't understand that life is a gift."

Sean took a swig from his beer, hoping to buy enough time to decide whether or not to agree with his friend. They had known each other for years. Had been roommates in college. They'd been to

strip clubs together. Gotten high together. Drunk together. Dosed
together. But they hadn't been spending much time together in the
last year or so. Not since Sean had gotten married and started a family.
Now his visits to Tony happened maybe once a month. Not even that
often anymore. Sean swigged his beer again and wondered how long
it took for someone to actually go crazy. Until he could come up with
an answer, he decided to play along.

"Yeah," he said. "I know what you mean."

"Give you an example," Tony said. "The other day, I was crossing
the street. Halfway through the crosswalk, this bleached blonde in
her tumor of an SUV pulls up to the stop sign. Now get this: I'm in
the crosswalk and she decides she's got time to go before I step in
front of her grille. So she does."

Sean shook his head. "Unbelievable," he said.

"But you know what?" Tony said. "I got her license plate. I know
where she lives. You want to come with me?" He was not laughing.

Sean swallowed air. "What about the grace of God?"

"I'm only kidding," Tony said, laughing now and waving his hand
like he was rubbing an invisible basketball. Sean had forgotten all
about that gesture. It meant Tony really wasn't kidding, but he was
claiming to so he could get away with what he was saying. He had
done it many times when they had been roommates. Tony would
insult Sean, then rub his invisible basketball and say, *I'm only kidding*.
"But seriously, people like that don't deserve to live. And sometimes I
think somebody should do something about it."

"Like you."

"Yeah, like me. If I thought I could get away with it, I would do it.
No question."

Sean tasted bile at the back of his throat and suddenly needed the
restroom. He stood up quickly.

"You okay?"

"Too much to drink, I think. Can't handle it the way I used to."

"You sure that's all it is?" Tony said as Sean rushed up the hallway and into the bathroom. "You're only on your third."

Sean closed the door and stood over the toilet. Another wave of nausea swept across his stomach, from left to right. The last thing Sean wanted was to throw up. Especially in here. The toilet bowl was covered with pubic hair plastered down by drying yellow urine. Sean had forgotten all about what it was like in a bachelor pad. He suddenly realized how much he had changed since he had met Lynne. How much more he had changed since Olivia had been born. What if Tony had changed that much, except in the opposite direction? He heard footsteps coming up the hall and reflexively locked the door.

"You okay, buddy?"

"Yeah. I'll be out in a minute."

"Good. I got something I want to show you."

Sean's mind leaped to the obvious possibilities: an axe, a gun, a straight razor. He suddenly wished he hadn't chugged the beer to buy himself time. He splashed cold water on his face and dried with what looked like a clean spot on the hand towel. Then he unlocked the door, opened it, and shut off the light.

The front room was empty. Outside the window behind Tony's chair, the street lamp was still off. The door to the garage, across the kitchen on Sean's left, was open. Cold air rushed at him from the black rectangle.

Sean heard footsteps behind him and turned around quickly. Tony was coming straight for him with a beer in one hand and a bong in the other. "So you know how it works?" he said as he pushed past Sean and hopped back into his chair.

"How what works?"

"Sit down, man. You're not thinking about leaving, are you?" He held up the bong. "Remember this?"

Sean nodded quickly. Smoking pot was something else he didn't do anymore. He looked at his watch. "It is getting kind of late."

"Come on. Sit down. You already passed."

"Passed?"

"The test. The way it works. Deciding who lives and who dies."

"Oh, right."

"See, I give a little test. I ask a question. If the person answers it right, they're free to go. If they answer it wrong: pffft." Tony drew his finger across his own throat. "Simple as that, baby. Simple as that."

Sean stared at Tony.

"See, someone like that lady who almost ran me over? I don't need to ask her the question. She just gets whacked. But take you, for instance. How would I know? Should I kill you or not? So I gave you my test."

"You did?"

"Yeah. The question I asked you: 'Did you ever think but for the grace of God you'd be a serial killer?'"

Sean laughed a little, like the bark of a small dog.

"People who say yes to that are the ones who deserve to die. Know what I mean?" Tony shook his head and loaded the bong. "I knew you'd pass, but I had to check anyway." He stopped and stared at Sean for a long time. Then he laughed crazily. "You should see the look on your face," he said. "Come on. You know me better than that. I'm only kidding." Then he waved his hand through the air, as if rubbing an invisible basketball.

Him

He came with the night
To our sleepy little town
Riding on long shadows
Growing blacker with the sundown

With a rattle and a shudder
He pulled to a halt
There in the square
With plans to sweeten the salt

For our town was poor
And milled with lost souls
Staring into their lives
On tables as empty bowls

With promises and smiles
He could and would fill them
Hiding all the while
His schemes to then kill them

Built of earth and tempered in fire
With joyless mirth he would sire
Nightmare's birth: sleep's black mire
The inescapable girth of him, the liar

Many fell in the coming days
Into his hand and deal
Getting what their hearts wished for
In exchange for his sign and seal

And soon one by one
They vanished with the setting sun
And when nearly all were done
Then did I run

I never looked back
Nor will there I travel
For in those final hours
I felt even my soul begin to unravel

Now I watch carefully
To keep where I am going
Gently reaping the fruits
Of this warning I am sowing

Ah, Sweet Moment
of Death

AH, SWEET MOMENT OF DEATH. PITY IT'S SO FLEETING.
Well, of course that's what's happening. Can't you feel it? The doctors must have lied, then. They do that. Don't want to put any undue stress on someone in an already fragile condition. Isn't that wonderful? Instead of giving people the chance to prepare, they snatch it away from them. No, I'm not a doctor. But you knew that, didn't you? Of course I'm familiar. You've spent your life in my company. That's right, no need to say anything. Recognize my voice now, don't you? Always thought it was your own.

Ever seen anyone die? They always get the same remarkable clarity of eye you've got right now. That look of seeing everything for the first time. Like me, for instance. Come on, you always knew I was with you, you just never believed it. And that was your *choice*, of course. Worked for me. I mean, most people these days don't believe. We work in secret, anyway, so disbelief only helps. Of course, it means I don't get to exercise some of my more, how to say, *interesting* tricks. But so be it. There is art in subtlety too, you know. Maybe my next assignment will be someone who does believe, and perhaps I will make him a magician. As they say: only time will tell.

Which reminds me, I can't stay long. I should be down in the maternity ward. Today is my next assignment's birthday and I hate to miss a good birth almost as much as I hate to miss a good death. All that pain. Ah, but I see I still have a few moments. Mind if I sit down? I will anyway.

Beautiful flowers, by the way. Your wife sent them? I'll make sure the hospital delivers them to the funeral parlor along with your body. No sense in throwing out perfectly good flowers.

Well, what to say? Hospital visits are always so awkward, aren't they? Especially for someone like you. People come in and you can see in their eyes that they're glad it's not them in that bed, all those nasty tubes and wires hanging out all over. And bedpans. Never such a horrid thing invented in the name of convenience. Terribly embarrassing, isn't it? How I love shame. Truly one of the finer emotions.

Feeling it a bit more now, are you? Heart swelling? Arteries bulging? Fit to burst open like a split persimmon and fill your insides? How I envy you humans your flesh. What's it like? Oh, never mind. Don't try to speak. I can see it's difficult for you. What's that, the call button? Can't quite reach it? Want me to push it for you? Don't be silly. And spoil this moment? Never.

Oh, please, don't look at me that way. Come now, let's reminisce. Let's think back to the finer times we had together. I must admit your life has had its moments. Overall a trifle boring, to be sure, but on several occasions, you were positively delightful. Like that Christmas we ruined for everyone because of your drinking. Now *that* was a party. You remember how we made your daughter cry? And then she got into a fight with her husband. And it wasn't long after that your sister died, was it? You never could remember those final days you'd had with her. That was one drawback. You forgot most of it. Practically wiped out any chance I had of overcoming you with regret. At least that time.

Not so when your baby girl died. Remember how we blamed your wife? How I love fits of passion. Heat of the moment. Yes, you regretted that. Still do, don't you? Let me tell you, that place was one of my favorites to go. Just to sit and languish in the cold dark where that memory lives. Tease it a bit, make it stir, just enough to remind you it's still there. All that psychoanalysis and still unresolved. Oh, I'll miss it.

What else? What else? If only I'd brought my scrapbook. We could look at it together. Oh my, is that the light in here or are you actually turning blue? No, it's you. I've never seen your eyes so big. That's it, go ahead and drool. It's so unbecoming.

You know what I just remembered? Your mistress. The first one. The redhead. What was her name? Not that it matters. But remember the time you took her to Las Vegas and you let her lose $1,000 of your money at the blackjack tables? And you hadn't even been drinking. How did we justify it? Love? That *was* it, wasn't it? Such a wonderful thing, love. Enables people to do so much they wouldn't consider otherwise. Remember how we went home and told your wife your wallet had been stolen? Those were some sweet times. Lying to your wife, lying to the credit card companies—all of them. You couldn't very well have claimed only one card had been stolen. Going to the Department of Motor Vehicles for a replacement license. Your insides were in absolute ribbons by the time that was all over. Pity you gave the girl up. If you'd stuck with her, you might have gotten a disease. And wouldn't that have been lovely.

My goodness, those veins in your neck are incredible. Hard to believe they haven't popped wide open already. Mind if I smoke? Of course you don't. Little late to worry about your health, no? Too bad you could never stick to those exercise programs. If only you'd lasted a bit longer, you might have gotten to the point where it felt good to exercise. But I made sure that didn't happen. You were always so easy to convince. Which was fine in a way. I sort of missed the struggles, though. Some of my other assignments have been such fierce fighters. Makes it a bit more challenging. A bit more of a laugh. They always gave up, of course, eventually. Always do. But I love a good fight.

I'm sorry, I'm rambling. I'm here to see you. Don't mean to talk about the others. How very gauche of me. Beautiful night out, isn't it? If you were up and around and back at home, it might be a fine night to start drinking again. Wait until the wife has gone to bed, then slip out to the corner bar for a quick one. All the sweeter because it's a secret. How I love secrets. Especially between married couples. The battle's almost won once I get people to start keeping secrets from each other.

And after you're gone, all of your secrets will be out. Think about that. Your wife going through all your belongings and papers. Think about all the things she'll find. Never did throw out that video you made with the other girl, did you? No. And that diary you kept for a while will make for some fine reading, won't it? I'm only sorry I won't be around to see it. New assignments always keep me so busy. Have to build up the enmity fast. But from what I understand about the new family, it's their first child and not one they wanted, so my workload might be light enough for me to get a few moments off and go see your wife some night.

Hey, careful there, you might tear the sheets pulling on them like that. Oh, please don't go yet. Can't you struggle a few moments longer? Try. Try to live. Oh, damn. I'm afraid I've taken it away, haven't I? Your reason to live. Nothing left now but the dark, you know. And the cold. If only you'd lit a few candles during your life instead of hurrying to snuff them all out every time you saw one burning. Oh well. Say hello for me when you get to the other side. Yes, you'll be able to talk again. Though you probably won't feel much like talking. New arrivals usually spend their time weeping and gnashing their teeth, stuff like that. Goodbye. Thanks for everything. Go ahead. Close your eyes. Let that last breath go. Let it go. Let it go. Ah, sweet moment of death.

Baby
Killer

Picture, if you will, a large house in a well-to-do suburb, set back from a narrow, winding, tree-lined street behind a low wall of natural stone. Take a closer look now at its grounds, at its expansive lawns, at the trickling, ivy-bordered creek that runs along the back fence, at the granny house tucked behind the rose garden and its carefully raked gravel paths, at the tennis court, the swimming pool, the four-car garage, the carport and the circular brick drive. Look inside, at its professionally decorated five bedrooms and three baths, at its walk-in linen closets, servants' quarters, formal dining room, game room; at the attic filled with sheet-covered furniture waiting for the children who grew up here to marry and get homes of their own. Look at the photos on the walls, of those same children, who went to expensive private schools and are now attending still more expensive private universities, children whose memories are of Christmases and birthdays packed with presents, whose high school graduations were marked by trips to Europe and new cars. Picture now the book-lined study on the second floor, and in it the father of those children, alone, sitting on the couch in the shadows, dressed, in spite of the cold, in only a robe and socks, one pale hand resting on a knee, the other now lifting a cigarette to his lips.

If you knew him, this would surprise you, for you would know that he quit smoking twenty years ago, after the birth of his first child. His stubble-covered face is slack, the corners of his mouth turned down. As if he doesn't want to, yet can't avoid it, he turns his head and looks at a closed door, its white face gray in the overcast winter-afternoon light. The movement of his head is stiff, as if invisible hands are forcing him to confront the door—or rather, what is beyond it. For behind the closed pale gray door is another door and behind it is another and behind it is the master bedroom, the gray light peering through the narrow slats of the Venetian blinds, spilling down in even lines over the unmade king-sized bed, the outline of the man's wife still pressed into its sheets and covers. It is her the man considers as he stares at the closed pale gray door. It is her he thinks about. Or rather, the argument they had five days ago, before she left, before he went to the study to sit on the couch, alone in the shadows, in the cold, to smoke and brood. How he had said he was sorry. How she had said sorry couldn't fix what had happened. How he had asked what he was supposed to do. How she had said there was nothing he could do. How she had fallen silent, forlorn. How he had hit the table. How she had quietly gone to the bedroom, her shoulders hunched, hiding her face from him even as she had closed the doors and packed her bags and gone downstairs to the four-car garage to drive her Mercedes onto the narrow, tree-lined street and away, leaving him in the dark, in the cold, alone with his thoughts. Alone to remember the cause of their argument. Alone to remember the accident. The one drink he'd allowed himself by way of celebration. The drive home. The sun in his eyes. The red light he'd not seen because of his faraway feel-good thoughts. The ball bouncing into the street. The child chasing after. Had the screams he'd heard even as he'd slammed on the brakes been the child's mother's or his own? Even now, after five days of replaying the accident over and over again, he still doesn't know. And how many times must he go through this anyway, he wonders? How long before it stops? Ever? Is the rest of his life doomed to this scene, repeating the accident to himself in its every inch of detail, replaying the argument with his wife in its every intonation? If only he hadn't broken six years of sobriety. If only he had driven home by a different route. If only the deal had fallen through so he wouldn't have had cause to celebrate. If only he'd stopped for gas. If only the child had not chased his ball. If only.

Now the man leans back and remembers how the child's mother had come to him in the emergency room to spit in his face and scream at him: "Baby killer! Baby killer!" How he had tried to say he was sorry, that he felt terrible, but she couldn't hear him, her screaming was so loud. He knows she was only thinking of her boy, her only child, the one she had tried five years to have, the one who had just learned to walk and talk and make his grandma laugh and his parents happy. The more he thinks about it, the more frustrated he becomes. The more frustrated he becomes, the more he wants to stop, and the more he wants to stop, the more he thinks about it and round and round he spins until the whirlpool of the scene he plays for himself sucks him into its dark heart and he hears the screams again and he asks himself, whose are they?

The thought occurs to him that he should get up and shower and get dressed and go back to work, and for the first time since his wife left, the man smiles. Then the smile fades as he realizes he'll only have to come home again. He'll only have to sleep and, sleeping, he will not be able to avoid dreaming the accident and, dreaming it, he will awaken and come to the study to the couch to sit, alone in the dark, in the cold, to think about it again.

Picture, if you will, a large house in a well-to-do suburb, set back from a narrow, winding, tree-lined street behind a low wall of natural stone. Take a closer look now at its grounds, at its expansive lawns, at the trickling, ivy-bordered creek that runs along the back fence, at the granny house tucked behind the rose garden and its carefully raked gravel paths, at the tennis court, the swimming pool, the four-car garage, the carport and the circular brick drive. Look inside, at its professionally decorated five bedrooms and three baths, at its walk-in linen closets, servants' quarters, formal dining room, game room; at the attic filled with sheet-covered furniture waiting for the children who grew up here to marry and get homes of their own. Picture now the book-lined study on the second floor, and in it the father of those children, alone, sitting on the couch in the shadows, dressed, in spite of the cold, in only a robe and socks, one pale hand resting on a knee, the other now lifting a gun to his head.

Her

WHAT DO YOU SEE? A YOUNG MAN. JUST OVER THIRTY. Small. Wiry. A bit bookish, perhaps, but no less appealing because of it. And you're thinking: how could *he* have done it? The answer is simple. I didn't. Not exactly. She did. I merely enabled her. Why? Love, of course. What other reason is there for anything we do? Certainly not hate. You may think people kill because they hate. But really, people kill because they love someone else more—themselves, perhaps, as is the case with self-defense. Oh, I know. What I did wasn't self-defense. No. But it was for love. A truer, purer love than any I have known. Or ever will, I'm sure. I loved her from the first moment I saw her. Standing next to my wife at the end of the drive looking up the wooded hillside, I loved her. Her clear eyes. Her smooth brow. Her vivid, black-topped head. Her wide yet delicate mouth. I was taken from that very moment, lifted out of myself. I had to have her. I wanted her right then. But my wife . . .

I could tell she didn't like her. From the way she wrinkled her pointed nose and pursed her fat mouth. But I wasn't about to let that stop me. Thinking about that moment now, perhaps it even fueled my desire, made me want her more. After my wife got back into the car, I stood outside a moment longer and looked up at her, wanting her. I knew then that she wanted me, too. And I nodded my head once as a promise that I would have her.

Back in town, we called the number we'd copied from the sign at the edge of the property. A woman's voice told me the realtor I was looking for was Tom Johansen. After a moment, he came on the line, his voice as rough as a freshly sawn piece of timber. I told him I was interested in a house and gave him the address. "The Wilson place?" he said. "You sure?"

I told him I was—very.

"Not from around here, are you?"

I told him my wife and I were from San Francisco, that I'd been appointed to a position as history of architecture professor at the university. This seemed to make some sense to him.

"Oh," he said. "I bet you like it."

"Yes," I said, again thinking of all her fine Victorian lines.

"Before I go to the trouble of showing you the place, there's a couple of things I want to make clear. First off, you're aware the house isn't finished?"

"Of course," I said. Even from the street, I had seen the exposed timbers at her rear. But what more perfect place for a young married couple to dream in? A place we could finish ourselves. Having a fixer-upper was a dream we'd discussed all through the time we'd struggled toward our PhDs.

"Okay. The other thing is there's been at least one murder there."

This took me by surprise, but it did nothing to color my picture of her. If anything, it lent an extra tang to my desire, like the first time my wife and I had experimented with handcuffs in bed. "At *least* one?" I repeated, unsure what the vagueness implied.

"Yeah, well, then there's the accidents. Ask me, I think those were murders too. Sheriff didn't think so. Course, what does he know? Off in the funny farm and all. Look, you still want to see the place?"

"Yes," I told him. "But do me a favor and keep quiet about the murder. My wife . . ." I let the sentence trail off, hoping the rest didn't need to be stated.

"Whatever you say. Ask me, though, you start keeping secrets, it's a sure way to get started on the road to divorce."

I shook my head at his advice, then arranged a time later in the afternoon for him to meet us. That settled, I hung up, paid the gas station attendant, and got back in the car.

"Our appointment's in two hours," I told my wife. "Hungry?" She nodded, so we set off in search of lunch.

All through the meal, I grew more impatient. Before I had seen her, I had been excited about my new job—our new jobs. I had thought a month too long to wait for the semester to begin. Now a month seemed nothing. Already I was thinking of only her. Like a schoolboy, my every thought turned back to her. You can imagine, then, how upset I was with the fact that my wife still seemed unsure. "Isn't it going to be too much work?" she asked, the first in a series of concerns stated as questions. Isn't it too far away from school? Isn't it too far from town? Had I not known better, I would have suspected she knew already of my feelings for her and was jealous. But she couldn't have known.

After lunch, we drove back up the hill. My wife thought an hour was too long to wait. She said we should be looking at other places. But I had already made up my mind. No matter the price, I was going to have her. I went out to walk around and get a better look. My wife wanted only to stay in the car and read. Too bad. We could have both loved her. She could have known the bliss that I knew. But I think she had already made up her mind, too.

When Johansen arrived, my wife's first question was about the price. Perhaps she'd hoped it would be too high. When Johansen quoted a price half of what we were willing to spend, I laughed hysterically. "You see?" I said. "This place was made for us." For me. I almost said "for me," but luckily, I caught myself. I told Johansen we had cash, and he was beside himself. The sale of our place in San Francisco had been good to us. As we signed the papers later in his stuffy, windowless office, I told my wife that the extra money would be more than enough to finish her the way she should be finished. Johansen was reluctant to give us the keys, but I told him he could call the bank for confirmation. Neither my wife nor I wanted to spend another night in the town's only motel. He handed over the keys and I drove as fast as I could, first back to the motel and then to her. I could hardly contain my excitement. I had fallen in love that afternoon and already I was spending my first night with her.

Imagine my surprise when we arrived after dark to find a single light on in the front room. My wife was concerned. Hadn't Johansen told us the electricity was off? "Maybe he got it turned on for us," I said. But I knew better. I knew then that she wanted me as badly as I wanted her and this was simply her way of welcoming me.

Inside the living room, we laid out the few belongings we had towed with us and got ready for bed. My wife was uneasy. She didn't like the fact that parts of the house were unfinished, open to the elements—and intruders—but for a few cheap sheets of plywood. I promised her there was nothing to worry about. This wasn't San Francisco, after all. She took a sleeping pill and was soon breathing heavily. I couldn't sleep. My excitement was too much. I wanted to get up and rush about and absorb every little corner of her, observe her every nuance. I was in love, and my whole being positively glowed with anticipation and excitement.

Sometime after midnight, I crawled out of my sleeping bag and went upstairs. In the master bedroom, which faced the ocean to the rear, I went onto the unfinished balcony and stared at the black headlands and moonlit sea. Then, overwhelmed with desire and unable to contain myself, I walked to the edge and slowly stroked the incomplete railings with a touch more tender than any I had ever bestowed on my wife. She came alive then, and returned my touches. She ran her hands along my bare legs and stroked my back and told me to close my eyes and let her do what she wanted. And I did. Within a few scant moments, I shuddered into her silken kisses and heard her laugh with delight at having made me feel so alive. My every limb buzzed in the afterglow. Even my teeth hurt. But the pain was sweeter than anything I'd known. Then I knew what I had to do. Indeed, what I had already started. And I nodded and touched her again and whispered, "Yes." She groaned with pleasure as I made my way back downstairs to the living room. My wife's sleeping bag was empty now, of course.

When I awoke the next morning, I was seized with that curious feeling of displacement that comes to all who awake for the first time in a new location. Then I realized where I was, and I relaxed again. Hoping against hope, I looked over and saw that I was indeed still alone. And I had that satisfaction that only comes to dreamers who wake to find their dreams are true.

I got up from the floor and made my way through the house, my smile growing with each step as my eyes lighted on all the changes. The entry hall finished; the kitchen floor tiled; the hallway to the spare room enclosed; and the balcony, complete. I stood there that morning and watched the ocean reflect the rising sun and knew this was what I'd been waiting for. We made love again and I napped afterward until a knock on the front door roused me.

It was Johansen. He had some paperwork for me to finish. I hesitated to let him in, but she opened the door herself and I knew then that everything would be all right.

Johansen was all business at first, until he saw the changes. He frowned at the kitchen floor and then looked at me. "You tile this already?" he asked.

"No," I said. "Was like that."

"No, it wasn't. I'm sure of it. And what about that? That hallway was nothing but frame yesterday, I'd swear it." When he faced me,

I could only watch as she engulfed him from behind. I shuddered. How could arms that had touched me so tenderly only hours before now be turned to this other, more horrible task? But I knew she was doing it for us, and that made it okay. She crushed him with her arms and then opened her mouth and swallowed him in a single gulp and I shook my head in disbelief that I, I alone, should have such a lover.

By the time I returned from driving Johansen's car over the cliff, the master bedroom was carpeted and painted. The windows were dressed in soft lace curtains so sexy I grew hard at the mere sight of them. "Oh, my love," I whispered to her. "Wait. Just wait."

No longer able to contain myself, I dressed and drove downhill as quickly as I could. On the outskirts of town, two blocks behind the motel where my wife and I had stayed, I pulled up to a collection of lean-tos under the bridge. A pair of ragged-looking men got up and stared at me. "What you want?" one of them asked. I told them I needed some help and if they were willing to work, I was willing to pay. I gave them $20 each to start and then drove the two of them back up the hill to her.

By the time sunset came, the master bedroom had a bed, the kitchen was complete, and not a single cross-member showed any- where. Our lovemaking that night was even more exquisite than it had been that morning, and I sensed that if only I could get her more, it would become even better. And I was right.

In the middle of the night, I got up again and drove downtown. I cruised past the pair of bars near the hospital and then decided I should go to the next town. No sense in being seen with too many vanishing people.

There, I met two girls. I might have found them attractive. Not now. I had to buy three rounds of drinks before they consented to come home with me. I hurried them inside when we got there and sat back to watch her feed. I had never imagined eating could be so beautiful. We made love again. And again.

The next morning, the sheriff and his deputy arrived. "No," I told them, I hadn't seen Johansen. Not since that first day. They asked to have a look around, and I let them—*she* let them. I sensed her hunger in the air like ozone after a lightning strike. She wanted them. And I knew why. These were strong young men, and I shuddered at the thought of what might happen after she'd had them. I wanted her to have them and I whispered for her to take them. But she let them go. They left, promising to be in touch again.

I departed minutes after they did. On the highway, I picked up a hitchhiking couple and their child. They were excited when I offered them a place to stay for the night. She took them even before they got inside. She laughed then, and told me how happy she was. No one had loved her like I loved her. And I told her she was right.

By the end of that first week, she was finished and furnished. Nothing I had seen in my life was as beautiful as her, and for the next few days we did nothing but make love and watch the sun rise from behind the mountains and set over the ocean.

The sheriff came back, of course. When he tried to take me, she took him, and when I went outside to drive his car over the cliff, I saw she had added another room to the south wing. But even as I returned to her and we made love under the rising moon, I knew it was over. She did, too. She woke me before dawn to say she had to leave. I knew what she meant. And she sensed that I knew. Yes, she told me, if I can't have you, I don't want anyone. I was flattered and saddened and as I walked out the front door and stood back, slow tears came.

I watched her stand—what a sight it was!—and shuffle to the cliff and hurl herself over the edge. I wanted to follow her. I would have if the deputy hadn't arrived and caught me.

Yes, staring at the black hole of his gun pointed at me, I thought about rushing him so he would have an excuse to end my life, but I knew that as long as I lived, she would live in me.

That is how I pass my time now, staring at the walls. But it's not concrete I see. No. It is her. And in the night, I dream of her and gently touch the love we shared. And I feed on it in my heart and it is enough. More than enough.

Unseen

I have seen the hidden web
That courses through every man
I have felt its tide and ebb
On dark beaches of black sand

I have performed on brimstone stages
For an audience of the dead
I have felt the spells of mages
And to their power I have been wed

I have seen the eyes of devils
And heard their crimson laughter
I have hitchhiked empty roads
And felt them chasing after

I have seen black, leathery wings
And heard their drumming tunes
I have felt their piercing talons
And seen their flesh-carved runes

I have known a man's soul departing
From his body under my blade
I have heard voices under earth
From lips rotten and decayed

I have been the moonless night
Over the land as a velvet cloak
I have been the red-hot iron of fear
That from your throat the scream did choke

I have felt the hangman's noose
Under hood round my veined neck
I have breathed my last
And been put at Death's call and beck

Yet when the sun does rise
And I awaken from this madness
To stare into my own eyes
And feel only blossoming sadness
At the hole below that ever widens
For the path my soul guidons
Into that dark city built of lies

Jonesy

JONESY WAS NEARLY OUT OF MONEY WHEN THE PHONE CALL came that he could have the apartment. He had been turned down so many times already that this call—from Mrs. Graves, even! the old-woman in the nice part of town—was an especial surprise. He told her he would be by that afternoon to sign the papers, drop off the deposit, and pick up the keys. She said that was fine, just fine. Then she said, "And by the way, I know about you." Jonesy felt his stomach go limp. *So that's it,* he thought. *A joke. Nothing more than a lousy joke. Tell me I can have the apartment and then tell me, oh wait, no, sorry, I made a mistake, no room for your type here.* At least the others had told him flat out.

"And," Mrs. Graves continued, "I also want you to know that it doesn't matter to me. I believe in giving people a second chance. My husband, God rest his soul, would have never been the man he came to be if he hadn't been given a second chance. He'd been in prison, too. Like you. For a short time. Nothing bad, mind you. Took some money from where he was working. But he probably would have turned into a regular criminal if he hadn't got caught so young. Thankfully, he changed his mind about what he wanted to do with his life. And double thanks there was someone around to let him do it."

Jonesy didn't know what to say, he was so surprised. He smiled for the first time since they'd let him out two weeks ago. Until now, there'd been nothing to smile about. "Well," he stumbled. "Thanks."

"You're welcome," said Mrs. Graves. "And by the way, what was it you did exactly?"

"Oh," he said, sucking in a breath. He didn't want to tell what he did. Telling got him in trouble. Even in there, telling had gotten him in trouble. From the way she'd said she knew about him, he figured she had already heard. But she hadn't. Or she wouldn't have asked. If he told her what he'd done, she'd change her mind about the apartment, he was sure of that.

"Mr. Jones?"

Jonesy bit his thumbnail. Then he remembered: his parole officer, the only person he knew to put into the space marked "References" on the applications for apartments, had said he wouldn't tell. And he'd said, "I think it would be good if you didn't, either. Robbery's one thing, but people can't . . . understand you. Know what I mean?" Jonesy had nodded in agreement. He nodded now at the memory and bit his thumbnail harder.

"Mr. Jones? Are you there?"

"I didn't mean to do it," he said quickly. "Really, I didn't." It was all he could think of—same as he'd told the jury seven years before.

"I'm sure you didn't," Mrs. Graves said. She hesitated another moment, waiting for him to tell her what he'd done. When the silence got too long, she said, "Well, it's not really any of my business anyway, is it?" She sounded disappointed.

Jonesy shook his head, then remembered she couldn't see him. "It was a long time ago," he said.

"I'm sure it was." She paused to give him one more chance to tell her. He didn't take it. "Well," she said, sounding disappointed again. "See you in a bit then, right?"

"Right," Jonesy said, relieved. When she said goodbye, he hung up quickly. Then he remembered: she'd said he could have the apartment. "Oh," he whispered, blowing out a breath. Then he said "Thankyouthankyouthankyou" to no one in particular and went to pack his bags. When he got to the apartment, Mrs. Graves told him she'd already taken care of the water, the electricity, and the gas. "If you want a phone," she said, "you'll have to see to that yourself." He thanked her again, then went upstairs, let himself in (with his own keys!), and threw down his bags. Before unpacking, he hurried downstairs and went up the street to the corner market, to use the phone booth there to call his parole officer, Mr. Inisheer, like he was supposed to. "I got an apartment," he said when Mr. Inisheer came on the line.

"You did? Oh, that's great, Jonesy. Furnished?"

"Yeah."

"Where?"

"On Twenty-Second Street."

"Is it okay? I mean, your SSI can cover it?"

"Oh, yeah. It's only a studio, so it's cheap. And the deposit was only two hundred dollars. Mrs. Graves—she's the landlady—she cut it down special for me. Said she wanted to give me a second chance."

"Oh, yes . . . I remember her," Mr. Inisheer said. "She called me for a reference. Told me the same thing. Said something about her husband had been in prison?"

"That's right," Jonesy said, excited. He liked his parole officer. Mr. Inisheer was a nice man.

"When can I come by and see it, then?"

"Anytime you want, Mr. Inisheer. Anytime you want."

"How about Monday, then? We're due for a meeting anyway. What say we do it at your place?"

"I'd like that."

"Me too. Okay. I'm glad to hear it. You'll be fine, Jonesy. Just fine. I know it. I can feel it. You're going to be all right."

Jonesy's smile got bigger, a sponge for Mr. Inisheer's watery praises. Whenever Mr. Inisheer told him he was going to make it, Jonesy believed. "Yeah," he said, "I can feel it, too."

"Great. I'll see you Monday after lunch, then. What's that address again?"

Jonesy gave it to him, then said goodbye. When he hung up, he was sure his face would split wide open from smiling so much.

That night, Jonesy changed into his pajamas and read awhile before turning out the light and closing his eyes. He thought about what he would do the next day and decided that first, he would go out to breakfast. Jonesy loved going out to breakfast. Of all the things he'd missed when he'd been in prison, going out to breakfast was the one he'd missed the most. Coffee and orange juice, then eggs and pancakes wrapped around sausages and bacon and ham and runny yolks and sourdough toast with lots of butter. *Yummy,* Jonesy thought and heard his stomach gurgle once. Then he remembered: he hadn't had any dinner. He'd been so excited by Mrs. Graves' phone call that afternoon that he'd forgotten all about eating. He'd go grocery shopping tomorrow. Right after he went out to break-fast. Jonesy went back to thinking about French toast and blueberry waffles with whipped cream and compote, but he was tired and soon fell asleep.

At first, his thoughts of breakfast turn into dreams of breakfast and he stands high above a table laden with plates full of breakfast food: everything he'd just paraded across his tired mind—and more. He knows it is all for him. And better yet, Mr. Inisheer and Mrs. Graves are paying for it. Slowly, he descends, as if falling from the sky, and when he lands, he sees that he is the size of a saltshaker on some giant's dining-room table. For a moment, he stands there in stunned disbelief. Then he remembers how hungry he is and he starts toward the plate of French toast. The pile of golden bread is twice his height and a waterfall of syrup and melted butter spills over the top edge. Jonesy licks his lips and leans forward and catches some on his tongue, the way he did with rain when he was young. *Oh*, thinks Jonesy, *surely this is heaven.*

But then behind him, a girl giggles sweetly, the sound (not that sound!) like bells in water. And Jonesy feels his stomach shrink: a fist squeezing a handful of air. He isn't hungry anymore, not for food. He turns around slowly and sees the girl. He doesn't want to see the girl, but he can't help it, his eyes are frozen. She stands on the edge of a rippling ice-blue pool. To one side, a table, an umbrella poking up from its center. Behind the pool, the house: a cliff wall of gray with a sliding glass door (a square of black) and some windows (more squares of black). The girl turns around, and her dark hair makes her look older than she is. The shadows in her face hide her youth. The widening hips and the budding breasts (the size of baseballs already!) say she is older. But best of all, Jones sees in her face that she hasn't found out the world is a bad place yet: she is young! Really young! Not fake young. And being young, she is happy. Really happy, not fake happy like the pills make him feel, but really happy, a happy Jonesy himself can only remember sometimes (like right when he wakes up and thinks he's still at home and his mom and dad are still alive). "Really young," Jonesy whispers, like a secret. He starts forward, wanting to grab her, to hold her, to hug her to him, to feel the happiness, but he bumps into a fence and falls away from the hole he is looking through. He realizes he has made a sound and he quietly but quickly gets back on his knees and looks through the hole in the fence and sees the young girl looking at him! He holds his breath and then she looks away and he sighs with relief and watches her again as she tugs at her swimsuit and jumps into the water.

"No," Jonesy says, and bites his thumbnail. He pulls his face away from the hole in the fence and puts his head in his hands. *No*, he tells himself. *Too young is a good thing, but not for that. Not for that!* And

when the girl's dad comes out of the house and jumps in the pool and
starts swimming after her, making her giggle, Jonesy plugs his ears.
That sound! Not that sound!

Jonesy woke, whimpering, his head under his pillow and his hands
clamped over his ears. He caught his breath and sat up. "No," he said
when he realized the dream was over. "A long time ago. All over now."
He remembered what Mr. Inisheer had told him the night before.
"That's right," he said out loud, "I'm going to be fine."

Still nodding, he swung out of bed and went to the bathroom.
He peed, then stripped off his pajamas and turned on the shower,
anxious to get under the hot water and wash the dream away. When
the room filled with steam, he went to the window over the toilet
and wheeled it open. As if he'd turned on a tap, the sound of giggling
children—like bells in water—poured through the window and into
his ears. Jonesy felt his stomach go limp. His heart beat faster. It was
a fake thing—it had to be. He was still dreaming. To make sure, he
climbed onto the toilet (the only way to see out the small window)
and peered through the screen, down to street level.

But there behind the building was a playground—not the dream
Jonesy had hoped for. It wasn't large, no bigger than a normal backyard, but it seemed literally blanketed with children, all of them
giggling and screaming and laughing. The top bar of the swing set
was tall—directly across from his window—and just as he saw this,
a girl reached the peak of her swing, her little black shoes and lacy
white socks so close Jonesy was sure he could touch them if he tried,
and her dress blew up and he saw a triangle of white cotton and
gasped and jumped off the toilet so quickly that he stumbled and
almost fell.

When he caught his balance, he clamped one hand over his terri-
fied mouth and started hyperventilating. "No," he said, and shook his
head and bit his thumbnail. *I can't stay here,* he thought.

Yes you can, said the other voice in his head, the one that always agreed with Mr. Inisheer. *Mr. Inisheer says you can make it. Besides, where else can you go? No one else would even give you an apartment.*

Jonesy bit his thumbnail harder while both voices fought to make themselves heard. And when the giggling broke through again, he hurried to the window and wheeled it shut as quickly as he could. He pressed the latch into place, then backed away and stared at the frosted pane of glass in terror.

After a moment, he realized: the sound was gone. Relieved, Jonesy went to the shower and shut it off. Now he could hear it again, and even though it wasn't nearly as loud as before, he hurried into the front room and closed the door. There, the sound was gone again. That was all there was to it, then: keep the door closed or the shower running. Then Jonesy told himself that the children wouldn't be out all day. It was probably some kind of school, so they would have to go inside sometimes. And besides, winter was starting. It had been raining Wednesday, when he'd first come by the apartment. Today's sunshine was just a break before a big storm. He'd heard that on the news yesterday. And when it rained, the children would have to stay inside. *And the place is probably closed on the weekends, too. And tomorrow's Saturday.*

Jonesy smiled. He felt completely calm. Mr. Inisheer was right. As long as he made himself calm, everything could be kept in control. When he wasn't calm, he wasn't in control, and things he didn't mean to do happened then. Well, he was calm now. *But,* he told himself, *I'll still have to be careful.* Nodding, Jonesy crossed the room and sat in the faded green chair by the window.

In spite of feeling calm, he ended up staying inside all day. He didn't mean to, it just happened. He thought about prison and how bad it had been in there for him, all the other men always beating up on him for what he'd done, calling him sick and saying he deserved to die. But he was the only one trying to make things straight in his head, really trying. The others were still bad. He'd seen them doing bad things to each other and stealing and selling drugs. He hadn't killed anybody. He hadn't even meant to do what he'd done. Some of the others had meant to do what they'd done. Even planned it. They were the sick ones. And they weren't even trying to get help. Not like Jonesy. He had seen the doctor three times a week and talked about his mom and dad and told all his secrets. He hadn't wanted to at first, but the doctor had told him it was the only way. "The only way to get to the spider, Mr. Jones, is to turn on the lights and sweep out the webs." That was what the doctor had said. But now the doctor was gone. Jonesy wasn't in prison anymore, and that's where the doctor was. He decided he should find a doctor out here to talk to.

When full dark finally filled the open space between the blinds, Jonesy decided he had better get up. He went into the bathroom and climbed onto the toilet and yanked the latch up and wheeled the window open. Hoping, he peered out and down and saw only a jagged diagonal of pale green light on the now-empty playground. Jonesy sighed in relief. He climbed down, then went to the shower and turned the water on.

After his shower, he felt much better. The hot water had washed away the icky stuff (the webs!) and had almost made him forget about the girl on the swing. As he got dressed, he remembered that he was in his own apartment, and a newfound strength filled him. Nobody was going to take this away, he decided. Nobody! He'd waited too long to get out on his own like this. He couldn't let anybody take it away.

When he checked his tie in the mirror, he thought for a moment that the face looking back at him was not his own. Then he realized he was smiling, and he wished his mother and father were with him. They would be proud, he was sure. Especially his mom, since she had always told him he wouldn't amount to anything, and here he was, amounting to something. *Well, almost,* he told himself. *Pretty soon. I'll get a job. Save some money. Maybe even get my own car someday.* Still smiling, he grabbed a jacket, then headed downstairs.

Outside, the air was thick with storm. The phone poles lining the street jutted up like corpseless crucifixes, the cables hanging between them black seams in the too-close sky. Jonesy thought surely if he reached up he could pull the sky open. The trees were stiff and black and empty, like silhouettes of trees more than real ones. The wind picked up and he smelled rain. He hoped it would come soon.

A block from his building, he turned left. He was thinking about breakfast again when he suddenly stopped in front of a sign that said "Happyhill Daycare—All Ages." Beyond the sign, the building lay quiet and dark, a sleeping beast, a coil of possibilities wound tight as a trap and ready to spring if touched. "A long time ago," he whispered, like an incantation. He backed away slowly, then turned and hurried up the sidewalk, back the way he'd come.

On Monday morning, Jonesy woke up feeling especially excited. Without having heard the sounds from next door all weekend, he had almost forgotten about them. More than that, though, today was the day Mr. Inisheer was going to come by and see his new apartment. Then he realized: if Mr. Inisheer found out about that daycare place, he wouldn't let him stay. Jonesy could understand why, but nothing had happened yet and he'd already been there for two days. He hadn't heard the sound at all and everything had been calm and in control. More than that, he'd really taken a liking to this little place. After that first day, things had changed. He had managed to get to the grocery store, and he'd had breakfast out—twice! He knew there was a reason he had waited so long to get back outside and on his own again. Now he knew how much he hated prison. What a terrible, sad place it was. What terrible, sad things it had done to him. Jonesy knew that. But he also knew that something lived inside him that had been killed in all the other people he had met inside that prison: hope. He really did believe that he was going to be okay. He was going to make it because he had hope. But he needed Mr. Inisheer to believe that. And he was suddenly afraid he wouldn't. (*Only if he finds out about the daycare, though,* Jonesy reminded himself. *What he doesn't know won't hurt him!*)

After lunch, the buzzer rang and Jonesy, still somewhat worried, went to open the door. Mr. Inisheer stepped inside, looked around. "Jonesy, this is terrific," he said.

Jonesy backed away, a big smile on his pale, pudgy face. "You really think so?"

"Oh, yeah. This is great."

Jonesy closed the door, half relieved. Mr. Inisheer sure didn't seem like he knew about the daycare.

"Why don't you give me the guided tour?"

Jonesy laughed and flicked his wrist at Mr. Inisheer. "Oh, go on," he said.

"Come on, really."

Jonesy shrugged and motioned with a swish of his heavy arm at the room behind him. "This is the living room and the bedroom. That couch over there folds into a bed." He stepped backward and motioned to the short hallway on his right. "Bathroom's through there at the end. Kitchen on the right."

Mr. Inisheer stepped forward and peered down the hall. "Very nice," he said. He faced Jonesy again. "Mind if I sit down?"

Jonesy shook his wide head. "Oh, no. No. Right over there," he said and pointed at the faded green chair by the window. Mr. Inisheer smiled and sat. Jonesy settled onto the couch on the other side of the room.

Mr. Inisheer smiled. "So how's it been going?"

"Good. Good."

"Been out much?"

"Yeah. Went out to breakfast twice since Friday. I wanted to go this morning too, but I figured I better eat what I got."

"You made it to the store, too?"

"Oh, yeah. Did that about first thing."

"You like it here."

"Oh," Jonesy said, blowing out a breath. "Yes. I don't think I ever want to go anywhere else."

Mr. Inisheer nodded and looked at the floor. "I'm afraid you'll have to," he said quietly.

Jonesy kept smiling, unsure what Mr. Inisheer meant. "What?" he asked.

Mr. Inisheer looked back up, his big brown eyes wide and open, like his face. "I said I'm afraid you'll have to. Go somewhere else."

"Where?" Jonesy said. He wasn't smiling anymore.

"No place particular. But somewhere other than here." He paused only a moment before explaining, "Mrs. Graves found out about you."

Jonesy nodded once, slowly. "Oh," he said.

"And of course she called me right away. Did you know about the school, Jonesy?"

"No," he said, frantic. He knew what Mr. Inisheer was thinking, and he didn't want him to think that. "No, I didn't. I swear. I didn't find out until after. I wasn't planning anything. I didn't even plan the first time. It just happened. I didn't mean for it to happen."

"I know, Jonesy. I know." Mr. Inisheer's voice was calm. He held his hand up like a crossing guard telling cars to stop, and Jonesy felt his heart get slower, as if Mr. Inisheer was making it slow down with his hand. He felt calm again.

"I'm sorry," he said.

"It's okay. I didn't think you knew about the school. Mrs. Graves did, however. She told me about how reticent you were on the phone."

"Reticent?"

"Not wanting to talk. Secretive. She said you were secretive about what you'd done."

"Because you told me not to tell."

"I know. I know. I told her that. And I explained to her my reasoning. She finally understood, but she still said she wanted you out of here. She wanted to do it Saturday, but I convinced her to let me take care of it."

"Thanks," Jonesy mumbled. He wished it had come out better because it was really what he felt, but he was sad, too.

"So I'll help you find another place. Meanwhile, you're going to have to go back to the motel."

"But couldn't you tell Mrs. Graves?"

"Tell her what?"

"Tell her what you tell me. That I can make it. That I'll be fine. I always believe you when you tell me."

Mr. Inisheer smiled. "I wish I could, Jonesy."

"But why can't you?"

"Because I don't think it's a good idea if you stay here."

Jonesy's pudgy face went slack. "So you don't think I can make it?"

"Yes," Mr. Inisheer said earnestly. "I do. But I think your staying here is a risk we shouldn't take. It's not a pressure you want to put on yourself."

"My doctor told me I have to face what I fear. The only way to get over a fear of heights is to climb a mountain. That's what he said."

Mr. Inisheer smiled weakly. "If it were up to me, I'd let you stay. But the building belongs to Mrs. Graves. If I don't move you out, she'll report me to my boss, and I could get in trouble. You don't want that, do you?"

"No."

"Okay. So why don't you get your stuff together and I'll take you back to the motel."

Jonesy nodded. He knew Mr. Inisheer would take care of him. But that Mrs. Graves wasn't a nice woman after all. Jonesy felt all traces of smile leave his face for good. His lips became a tight line as he stood and went to the closet. He shoved his clothes into his suitcase and put his books in a brown paper shopping bag he had saved from the store.

"Is that it?" Mr. Inisheer asked.

Jonesy nodded and followed Mr. Inisheer down to his car.

At the motel, Mr. Inisheer checked him in and paid for his room, a week's worth. Jonesy thought that was very nice. Mr. Inisheer said it was the least he could do, because he felt bad about the apartment. "We'll find you another," Mr. Inisheer said. "And I'll bet it'll be better than the one you had."

"You really think so?" Jonesy asked.

Mr. Inisheer nodded and handed Jonesy the keys to his room. "I've got some things to take care of tomorrow. But I'll come over on Wednesday and pick you up and we'll have lunch and look for an apartment. How would that be?"

"Fine," Jonesy said. He waved when Mr. Inisheer went to his car and drove out of the parking lot.

Still smiling, Jonesy let himself into his room and set his bags down. He looked around and suddenly realized where he was: back in the motel. *Might as well be back in prison,* Jonesy thought, his smile fading away. He hated the motel. Hated it. Especially now. Especially since he'd been in his own apartment. Jonesy shook his head and thought about Mrs. Graves and all her talk about giving people a second chance and being so nice and all she turned out to be was a big fat liar. Exactly like his mom and his dad and his lawyer and everyone else he'd ever met. Except Mr. Inisheer, of course. At least, Jonesy didn't think he was a liar. *But what if he is?* asked the voice in his head, the one that never agreed with Mr. Inisheer, the one that told him about how good it felt to do the bad things.

"He's not," Jonesy said out loud, stamping his foot on the floor. Sad and disappointed, he turned the TV on and sat on the bed.

Later, he realized he was hungry, and without thinking, he stood up and started toward the kitchen. Then he remembered: he wasn't in his apartment anymore. And he'd forgotten his food! All the food he'd bought at the store and it was back in his apartment. *No,* Jonesy thought. *Not mine anymore. But that food is.* He decided he should go get it. He thought about waiting until Wednesday, when Mr. Inisheer was coming back, but a lot of it would have gone bad by then. *No,* he thought, *I better go get it now.*

Outside, the sun had set and the sky was a sheet of dark gray. Jonesy hoped it wouldn't rain, because he didn't have an umbrella. He locked his door carefully, then went downstairs and walked to the bus stop on the corner.

The bus came and soon he was downtown, off the bus and on his way home. Then he remembered: it wasn't his home anymore, and he got more upset with every step. Darn that old Mrs. Graves! All her talk about giving people a second chance and she was nothing but a big fat liar. *And liars burn in hell,* his mother's voice whispered in his head.

"That's right," Jonesy said out loud. He had never lied. Not after his mom had told him that. He had only done that one bad thing, and even that he hadn't meant to do. It had just happened.

At the apartment building, he rang Mrs. Graves' bell and stepped back. A minute later, he heard the deadbolt click, and the door opened to the chain. Mrs. Graves looked out, her gray face dark. Yellow light from inside showed all around her.

"Mr. Jones?" she said. "What are you doing here?"

"I forgot my food," he said. "I got hungry and then I remembered I forgot my food."

"You'll have to come back tomorrow," she said. "I'm busy." She started to close the door, but Jonesy stopped it with his hand. She looked up at him, her eyes wide. He knew she was afraid. He didn't know why. He never knew why people were afraid of him. They didn't have any reason to be. He took his hand away.

"But it's my food and I'm hungry."

"Don't you have any more money?"

"I have to save it."

"Where's your parole officer? Did he bring you here?"

"No."

She looked at him again. "All right," she said. "Let me get the key." She closed the door. Jonesy shook his head and frowned. *Why are people so mean?* he wondered.

Nothing but a big fat liar, said the voice in his head, the one that never agreed with Mr. Inisheer, the one that told him about the bad things.

"Yeah," Jonesy said out loud, and then the door opened and Mrs. Graves came out, staring at him, one hand in the pocket of the coat she had put on.

"Well, hurry up, damn it," she said. "Let's go. I haven't got all night." She went past Jonesy quickly and up the stairs. He followed.

She unlocked the door of the apartment and stood back. Jonesy walked past her, not looking at her, and went in. He looked around and suddenly felt like crying. *This was mine,* he thought. *Only now it's been taken away.* Mrs. Graves told him to hurry up again and he went into the kitchen. He found a paper bag under the sink and unfolded it, then opened the refrigerator and started taking his food out. As he did, he began to cry. He didn't want to, but he couldn't help it.

"What is going on in here?" Mrs. Graves said.

Jonesy looked up and saw her standing in the doorway, one hand still in her coat pocket, the other clutching the keys. "Why are you so mean to me?" Jonesy shouted at her.

She jerked her head back and laughed. "Me? Mean to you? Suppose that's one way of looking at it. I prefer to think of it as doing those children next door a favor. God only knows what might have happened."

"Nothing!" Jonesy shouted. "That's what would have happened."

"Sure. That's what you say. But I know about your type. Can't help yourself."

"Oh yes I can. I found this apartment by myself. I went to the store myself. I was fine until you had to go and ruin everything. You big fat liar."

Jonesy stood up suddenly, and Mrs. Graves jumped back. The hand in her coat pocket flew out and Jonesy saw she had a knife. Her knuckles were white around its wooden handle. The blade glinted dully. "Stay back, you," she said, her voice trembling. "Get out of here now. Take your damned food and get out of my building! Should have never let you in here in the first place. Go on!"

Jonesy hung his head. He wasn't crying anymore. He was mad now. And the voice in his head told him how good it would feel to hurt Mrs. Graves, to make her feel the way she made him feel.

No, said the other voice, the one that always agreed with Mr. Inisheer, the one the doctor had told him to always listen to. But Jonesy couldn't hear it. All he could think about was hurting Mrs. Graves. He reached down and picked up a big can of chicken soup. "You big fat liar!" he screamed, and threw the can at her. It struck her in the head with a dull crack, and she fell backwards. The knife flew from her hand and her forehead opened and blood spilled out and stained the carpet.

Jonesy stood still, the silence in the room suddenly terrible in its size.

"What the hell?" someone said, and Jonesy looked up and saw a man in the doorway.

"I didn't mean to do it," he said. "Really. But she made me. She didn't believe in me. She's nothing but a big fat liar, that's what she is."

The man ran away, and Jonesy hung his head. He knew there was nothing he could do now. Nothing but wait. They would come for him soon. Like they had before, after the first bad thing. And they would take him away to prison again. "Oh," he said, blowing out a breath as he sat down on the kitchen floor to wait.

Writer's Block

THE FIRST THING FRANK NOTICED WAS THE MAN'S SHIRT. That's because what this guy was wearing hardly qualified as one. It was made of black netting and cut in half so that his entire midriff was exposed. Frank thought the man should have been embarrassed by what the shirt revealed (tattoos on too-pale skin and nipple rings). That he was not convinced Frank the man had worn this particular shirt precisely because its flamboyance clashed with the regimental atmosphere of the post office where they both now stood in line. Obviously, this was a man who wanted to be looked at. Judging by the glances of those around him, his desire was being amply fulfilled.

Because he was a writer and had long held a fascination with people who lived on the fringes of "normal" society, Frank continued staring. These outsiders (as he called them) often inspired stories, such as the one he had based on the homeless woman who rode around his neighborhood on a bike laden with doll parts. The man in the net shirt fascinated Frank in the same way, and he began to think there might be a story in this encounter. He certainly hoped so. He had been battling writer's block for the last three weeks, and his publisher was pressuring him to finish his latest short story collection. Ironically, he needed only one more tale.

Frank turned his attention back to the man in the net shirt and began collecting details. His arms were pale and thin, loaded with a dozen small parcels carefully wrapped in brown paper and covered with red, white, and blue priority mail stickers. Frank speculated the man had a home business of some kind, selling products through the mail. He wasn't sure why he thought this. The assumption simply felt correct, in spite of (or perhaps because of) the fact that the packages were all different sizes.

As the man went to the counter, he passed Frank close enough for him to notice that his eyebrows had been plucked, his arms shaved, and his shoulder-length blond hair bleached so many times it now looked like ancient straw. These feminine details seemed in direct opposition to the masculine tattoos and nipple rings, but before Frank had any time to consider this, another window opened and the clerk called him forward.

Frank finished his own business immediately after the man in the net shirt so that the two of them left the building at the same time, although through separate doors. As Frank walked to his car, he searched the parking lot until he saw the man get into a cream-colored Lexus and drive away. The affluence suggested by the car surprised him. If anything, the man had struck him as someone on the lower end of the income scale. Then again, he had also struck him as the sort of person who wouldn't have much business at the post office. Frank got into his own car and drove home to see if he could spin a story out of the man in the net shirt.

Three days later, Frank had only gotten as far as describing the initial encounter in the post office. Writer's block had set in again. He was almost ready to give up on the idea when, driving to the grocery store, he looked in his rear-view mirror and saw the man from the post office behind him. Only this time, the man was not wearing his net shirt. In fact, he was no longer a man. Frank quickly lifted his foot off the gas, and as the cream-colored Lexus pulled up alongside him, he saw fingers tipped with pink nails lift a cigarette to a mouth painted with dark red lipstick. Frank changed lanes and fell in behind him, convinced that fate had put this man back in his path. Perhaps this was the development that would restart his story.

He followed the man at a careful distance, the trip to the grocery store now forgotten, and grew more nervous when the man not only drove into Frank's neighborhood but even turned down Harwood—the street where he lived. Frank suddenly feared the man had been following *him* since their encounter in the post office and was going to tease him with this display of knowledge. Instead, the man pulled to a stop in front of a corner house only three blocks from his own. Relieved (and hardly able to believe his luck), Frank hurried home, parked the car, and immediately went out for his evening walk, changing his usual path so that he now passed the man's house.

Although it was not well kept, overt signs of wealth surrounded it: a speedboat under a gray tarp parked in an enclosed driveway on one side, a pair of jet skis on a trailer, and in the open garage, an older-model BMW, its windows dusty with age and disuse. Frank also noticed the flagpole rising up behind the house, bearing both the American flag and the black POW/MIA banner. Another assumption suddenly struck Frank: this man was a Vietnam veteran who had been so traumatized by his wartime experiences that he had become someone else. As he passed the Lexus, he noticed the back seat was filled with the same kind of packages he had seen in the man's arms that first day at the post office. This seemed to confirm his initial suspicion about some kind of home-based business. He was tempted to see if he could read one of the return address labels, but he thought better of it and continued to the next corner. His excitement mounted as he crossed the street and walked past the house again on the opposite side. *Maybe there's more than a short story in this particular outsider,* he thought. He noted the house number—219—and hurried home.

In his office, he turned on the computer, connected to the Internet, and entered the man's address in the reverse phone directory. Immediately, he had a name—M. Peltier—and a telephone number. He jotted the information on one of the yellow index cards he kept for story ideas and switched to a public-records website. He discovered the M. stood for Mary and that she was fifty-two years old. This would have made her eighteen in the early 1970s, an ideal candidate for the draft. He punched the full name into several other search engines but found no references.

Frank took the tennis ball from the top of his computer monitor and leaned back in his chair. He tossed the ball back and forth from one hand to the other as he considered what he had so far. The information proved nothing, of course. The man might not even be Mary Peltier. Perhaps he rented his house and Mary was the owner's name. Maybe he could call her and pretend he was looking for someone named Mary Peltier. He would have to use a pay phone to ensure he couldn't be traced with caller ID. But it might work.

He dropped the tennis ball, then grabbed a handful of change along with the yellow index card and left the house. There was a pay phone at the city office building on Main Street, two blocks away.

Ten minutes later, he deposited two quarters and dialed the number, then held his breath as Mary Peltier's phone started ringing. He braced himself, ready to launch into the "looking for my high school sweetheart" routine he had come up with on his way over. After three rings, he anticipated a machine. After six rings, his anticipation shifted to disappointment. She didn't even have an answering machine. He let it ring a dozen times to be sure, then hung up.

Back home, Frank returned to his office and found his writer's block had left him. He wrote about seeing the man in traffic and following him to his house. Frank had, of course, created a fictional alter ego for this tale: a writer with writer's block, trying to write one last story for his short story collection. He liked the way it was coming together, until his writer's block returned, right as he got to the part of the story where he—the writer, rather—had called Mary Peltier's number and gotten no answer.

He went to the garage and rummaged through his old fishing gear until he found a small pair of binoculars. He took them onto the front porch and confirmed what he had suspected while standing at the pay phone: if he positioned himself just right, he could actually see number 219 from his own house. What especially shocked him, however, was that he saw her, getting out of the cream-colored Lexus, swinging her large black purse over one shoulder, and strolling up the front walk. Frank had barely registered the color of her skirt and blouse (brown and beige) before she disappeared behind a large tree that blocked his view of her front door. When he lowered the binoculars, he glanced across the street and saw his neighbor through her front window. Her TV was on, but she was looking directly at him. He laughed at how absurd he must look, but then realized it wouldn't be so funny if she called the police and told them he was spying on her. *God, no,* Frank thought as he went back inside and quickly closed the door. What could he possibly say? "Excuse me, miss, but I wanted to let you know that I wasn't looking at you with my binoculars. I was watching the transvestite up the street." He let loose another peal of absurd laughter and hurried back to his office to add all this to his story.

When he finished, bringing his alter ego up to the moment when he laughed absurdly at his situation and then went back to his office to add to the story, he returned to the front porch for another look at number 219. As soon as he opened the front door, he saw his neighbor across the street, now sitting on her own front porch, reading. He closed the door quickly and leaned his back against it. He realized he had two choices. He could stop where he was and simply make up the rest of the story, or he could continue this transcription of his real investigation of Mary Peltier. Even as he stepped away from the door, he knew the answer. He could never make up something better than the truth of the man who lived in number 219. He thought he should try, just to be sure, but even before he made it to his office he gave up that idea as well.

The next day, he parked a block from number 219 and watched in the rear-view mirror, waiting for Mary to show herself. Around 9:30, she did, only she was a he once again. He was wearing the same thing he had been the first time Frank had seen him: the cut-off jean shorts, the tennis shoes with no socks, and the net shirt. He had half a dozen packages in his arms, which he put in the back seat, then he got behind the wheel. As the cream-colored Lexus headed toward Main Street, Frank followed at a careful distance.

Fifteen minutes later, the Lexus pulled into the parking lot of a strip mall on Center Street, a few blocks from the freeway. The lot was too small for Frank to follow without being noticed, so he drove past and made the first left turn he could. He swung into a U-turn on the side street, then headed back up Center to the strip mall, pulled in, and parked facing the street. He adjusted his rear-view mirror, scanning the row of shops behind him. A liquor store, a used bookstore, a vacant storefront, and then a used clothing store called Mary's Closet. The Lexus was parked in front, and Mary (if that was indeed his name) was taking the load of boxes from the car to the front door. Only then did Frank notice that the sign in the window said the store was closed. Mary unlocked the door with a key on a fluffy pink key chain, then slipped through and closed it quickly behind him.

Frank took out his cell phone and checked the time. Almost 10:00. A few minutes later, Mary appeared at the window, turned the sign around to "Open," and unlocked the door again. Frank waited as long as he could, then got out of the car and headed toward the store.

The place was like a costume shop for a 1950s musical: all sequins and feathers and colors so bright they made Frank's eyes hurt. The door swung shut behind him and the bell rang again. Even though the counter was unoccupied, Frank quickly touched a few things on the nearest rack to at least give the impression he was a real customer. Good thing, too, because Mary came through a thick curtain of beads and headed straight for him.

"Help you find something?" he asked in a voice as rough as eighty-grit sandpaper.

Frank was shocked. He had expected some kind of swishy whisper, not something that belonged on the cigar-stained lips of a construction foreman.

"Uhhm," Frank started, even more shocked that he was completely out of words. *A fine state for a writer to be in,* he thought, his mouth still hanging open. "I'm going to a costume party," he finally blurted, and Mary cocked his head back, offended.

"I only sell real life here, honey. Try Julianne's on East Eighteenth. She'll have something for you."

Mary started to turn away. By the time Frank knew what he was doing, it was too late—his hand was already on her shoulder. Mary stopped and turned around, his eyes blazing so brightly that Frank yanked his hand back as if it had been burned. He backed up a little too, until hangers covered with feather boas poked him in the back like a stick-up man's pistols.

"Who are you?" Mary growled.

"What do you mean?" Frank said, trying to keep his voice from shaking.

"You're not looking for a costume."

Frank tried to smile, but Mary plowed ahead, taking a step forward. The hangers poked Frank in the back again.

"I've seen you before. Somewhere."

"Maybe."

"No," Mary said, suddenly growing sure. "I have seen you. Are you following me?"

"No."

"You are. What are you? Some kind of detective? Did Robby hire you?"

"No. I swear."

"I don't believe you," Mary said as he grabbed Frank by the shirt collar and twisted it tightly.

"I live near you," Frank said through a cough.

Mary's lip, turned up in a sneer, suddenly relaxed a little. "Where?"

"On Harwood. I'm five thirty-two."

Mary let his shirt collar go and turned away. "So what are you doing in here?"

"I wanted to see what it was you did. I saw you in the post office with all those packages and . . ."

"So you *did* follow me?"

"Not exactly."

"What, then?"

"Then I saw you. Driving. Here."

Even as he typed it, Mary realized this ending wasn't going to work, either.

With a sigh of frustration, he stood up from the computer and grabbed the pack of cigarettes off his desk. He lit one and walked to the window. He parted the shades, picked up the binoculars, and aimed them down the street at number 532. That was where he lived. The little weasel who had stared him down in the post office. He had decided to call him Frank. And he had known from the moment he'd seen the way the guy had looked at him that there was a story in there somewhere. There had to be. And he had to find it soon because his deadline was past and his publisher would be calling. Again. Asking when he was going to finish the story collection.

He put the binoculars back down and took another drag from his cigarette. He scratched his nipple ring and noticed that the polish on two of his nails was chipped.

He stubbed the cigarette out and sat back down at his desk. He stared at the screen, trying to imagine what a weasel like Frank would really be all about. And then he saw it, clear as day. He moved the mouse and clicked the cursor in at the point where Frank got out of the car and headed toward the store. Only this time, he put a gun in his pocket.

"Yeah," Mary whispered. "Maybe that'll do it."

The Pale, Unkempt Hours
of Late Gray Afternoons

I

In lines we wait
And in standard squares we turn
The circles of our days.

By weeks we count
The years of our youth
As they slip away.

And then,
When pictures from days gone
Like water to the sea
Whisper past
On silken feet
(The sound of spiders spinning patiently)

And when the pale, unkempt hours
Of late gray afternoons

Trade skin for skin
In the slanting darkness
Of our gloom
And we are filled

With empty spaces

Lined with black
And ice-green light
A slow-motion photograph
Of slanting drops.

We all wander
Like some hunted beast awakened.
We track the mask of memory
And its path leads us
Where, dim,
The orange and purple rainlight
Glides in silent sheets
Across black concrete.

The tears of the city
Are shed for me
And for many.

Some seek solace in silken flesh.
Some in the spinning din.
But I am the revenant,
Here.

II

At a doorless threshold I stand
At a gate of unseen stone
And behind me fall the ordered lines
Of a thousand broken dreams
Another thousand broken bones.

Before me,
Against a hanging curtain of gray
Birds like black leaves
Bloom on bare trees
And fall again
To fly away.

Here,
Where the sound of water
Like air in a still, cold shell
Slips through me

Like a snake
Banded with shadows
Its scales rippling glass,
The river
Shows my face
And the madness of my sanity.

These granite words
Tumble from my lips.

In blocks they wait
For the chisel to chip.
And I wonder:

When does where I am now
Become
Where I was then
When does
Where I am now
Become
Where I was then?